TUNNEL OF BONES

VICTORIA SCHWAB

SCHOLASTIC

Scholastic Children's Books
An imprint of Scholastic Ltd
Euston House, 24 Eversholt Street, London, NW1 1DB, UK
Registered office: Westfield Road, Southam, Warwickshire, CV47 0RA
SCHOLASTIC and associated logos are trademarks and/or
registered trademarks of Scholastic Inc.

First published in the US by Scholastic Inc, 2019
First published in the UK by Scholastic Ltd, 2019

ISBN 978 1407 19693 0

A CIP catalogue record for this book
is available from the British Library.

Printed by CPI Group (UK) Ltd, Croydon, CR0 4YY
Papers used by Scholastic Children's Books are made
from wood grown in sustainable forests.

1 3 5 7 9 10 8 6 4 2

This is a work of fiction. Names, characters, places, incidents
and dialogues are products of the author's imagination or are used
fictitiously. Any resemblance to actual people, living or dead,
events or locales is entirely coincidental.

www.scholastic.co.uk

TO MY FAMILY, SOMETIMES FAR,
BUT ALWAYS CLOSE

THE PAST IS A VERY DETERMINED
GHOST, HAUNTING EVERY CHANCE
IT GETS.

—*Laura Miller*

CASSIDY'S MAP OF
PARIS, FRANCE

Boulevard Haussmann

Place de
l'Étoile

Place de
l'Opéra

JARDIN DES TUILERIES

Rue de

Quai Branly

Les
Invalides

Champ
de Mars

Boulevard

THE LOUVRE

EIFFEL TOWER

Boulevard du Montparnasse

Boulevard de Vaugirard

Place
Denfert-Rochereau

Boulevard S

THE CATACOMBS

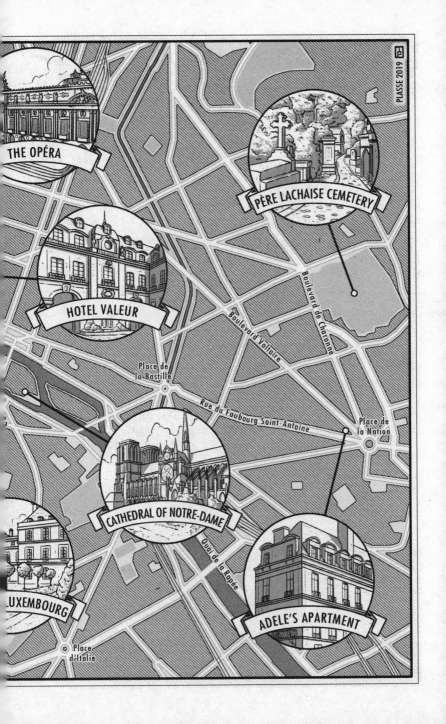

THE OPÉRA

PÈRE LACHAISE CEMETERY

HOTEL VALEUR

Boulevard Voltaire

Boulevard de Charonne

Place de
la Bastille

Rue du Faubourg Saint-Antoine

Place de
la Nation

CATHEDRAL OF NOTRE-DAME

Quai de la Rapée

LUXEMBOURG

ADELE'S APARTMENT

Place
d'Italie

PLASSE 2019

PART ONE

CITY OF LIGHT

CHAPTER ONE

The train rattles as it moves beneath the city.

Shadows rush past the windows, little more than streaks of movement, dark on dark. I can feel the ebb and flow of the Veil, the drumbeat of ghosts on every side.

"Well, that's a pleasant thought," says my best friend, Jacob, shoving his hands into his pockets.

"Scaredy-cat," I whisper back, as if I'm not also creeped out by the presence of so many spirits.

Speaking of cats, Grim scowls up at me from the cat carrier in my lap, his green eyes promising revenge for his current imprisonment. Mom and Dad sit across from us with their luggage. There's a map of the Metro above their heads, but it just looks like a tangle of colored lines: more like a maze than a guide. I went to New York City with my parents once, and we rode the subway every day, and I still couldn't tell where we were going.

And that time, everything was in English.

Jacob leans against the wall beside me, and I look out the window again. I study my reflection in the glass—messy brown hair, brown eyes, round face, and the old-fashioned camera around my neck—but the space next to me, where Jacob should be, is empty.

I guess I should explain: Jacob is what he likes to call "corporeally challenged." Basically, he's a ghost. No one can see him, except for me. (And a girl we just met named Lara, but that's only because she's like me, or I'm like her, someone who's crossed the line between the living and the dead, and made it back.) If it seems strange, the whole dead-best-friend thing, well, it is, but it's not the strangest thing in my life by far.

My name is Cassidy Blake, and one year ago, I almost drowned. Jacob saved my life, and ever since, I've been able to cross into the Veil, a place filled with the spirits of the restless dead. It's my job to send them on.

Jacob scowls at that. "Your job, according to *Lara*."

I forgot to mention that Jacob can read my mind. Apparently that's what happens when a ghost pulls a human back from the brink of death—things get kind of tangled up. And if being haunted by a psychic dead boy isn't weird

2

enough, the only reason we're here on this train is that my parents are filming a reality TV show about the world's most haunted cities.

See?

The fact that Jacob is a ghost is starting to seem normal.

"*Para*normal," he says with a crooked grin.

I roll my eyes as the train slows, and a voice on the intercom announces the station.

"Concorde."

"That's us," says Mom, bouncing to her feet.

The train pulls to a stop and we get off, making our way through the crowds of people. I'm relieved when Dad takes Grim's carrier—that cat is heavier than he looks—and we haul ourselves and our suitcases up the stairs.

When we reach the street, I stop, breathless not from the climb but from the sight in front of me. We're standing at the edge of a *massive* square. A circle, really, surrounded by pale stone buildings that reflect the late-afternoon light. Gold trim shines on every surface, from the sidewalk rails to lampposts, fountains to balconies, and in the distance, the Eiffel Tower rises like a steel spear.

Mom spreads her arms, as if she can catch the whole city in one giant hug.

"Welcome to Paris."

You might think a city is a city is a city.

But you'd be wrong. We came from Edinburgh, Scotland, a nest of heavy stones and narrow roads, the kind of place that always feels cast in shadow.

But Paris?

Paris is sprawling and elegant and bright.

Now that we're aboveground, the drumbeat of ghosts has receded, and the Veil is just a light touch against my skin, a flicker of gray at the edge of my sight. Maybe Paris isn't as haunted as Edinburgh is. Maybe—

But we wouldn't *be* here if that were true.

My parents don't follow fairy tales.

They follow ghost stories.

"This way," says Dad, and we set off down a broad avenue called Rue de Rivoli, a street lined with fancy shops on one side and trees on the other.

People bustle past us in chic suits and high heels. Two

teenagers lean against a wall: The guy has his hands in the pockets of his black skinny jeans, and the girl wears a silk shirt with a bow at her throat, looking like she stepped straight off a fashion site. We pass by another girl in glittering ballet flats and a boy in a striped polo shirt walking a poodle. Even the *dogs* are perfectly styled and groomed here.

I look down at myself, feeling suddenly underdressed in my purple T-shirt, my gray stretchy pants, and my sneakers.

Jacob only has one look: His blond hair is always tousled, his superhero T-shirt always creased, his dark jeans worn through at the knees, and his shoes so scuffed I can't tell what color they used to be.

Jacob shrugs. "I do me," he says, clearly unbothered.

But it's easy not to care what other people think when none of them can *see* you.

I lift my camera and peer through the cracked viewfinder at the Paris sidewalk. The camera is an old manual, loaded with black-and-white film. It was vintage even before we both took a plunge into an icy river back home in upstate New York. And then, in Scotland, the camera got thrown against a tombstone, and the lens shattered. A very nice lady in a photo shop gave me a replacement, but the new lens has a swirl, like a thumbprint, in the middle of the glass—just one more imperfection to add to the list.

What makes the camera truly special, though, is how it works *beyond* the Veil: It captures a piece of the other side. It doesn't see as well as *I* do, but it definitely sees more than it should. A shadow of the shadow world.

I'm just lowering the camera when my phone chimes in my pocket.

It's a text from Lara.

Lara Chowdhury and I crossed paths back in Edinburgh. We're the same age, but it's safe to say she's years ahead in the whole ghost-hunting department. It helps that she spends her summers hanging out with the spirit of her dead uncle, who happens—happen*ed*—to know about all things supernatural. *He* wasn't an in-betweener (that's what Lara calls people like us), just a man with a large library and a morbid hobby.

Lara:
Gotten yourself in trouble yet?

Me:
Define trouble.

Lara:
Cassidy Blake.

I can practically hear the annoyance in her posh English accent.

Me:
I just got here.
Give me a little credit.

Lara:
That isn't an answer.

I lift the phone, make a goofy grin, and snap a photo of myself giving a thumbs-up on the crowded street. Jacob's in the frame, but of course he doesn't show up in the photo.

Me:
Jacob and I say hi.

"*You* say hi," he grumbles, reading over my shoulder. "I have nothing to say to *her*."

Right on cue, Lara snaps back with her own reply.

Lara:
Tell the ghost to move along.

"Ah, here we are," says Mom, nodding at a hotel just ahead. I tuck my phone back in my pocket and look up.

The entrance is ornate—beveled glass, a rug on the curb, and a marquee announcing the name: HOTEL VALEUR. A man in a suit holds open the door, and we step through.

Some places just scream haunted . . . but this isn't one of them.

We move through a large polished lobby, all marble and gold. There are columns, and bouquets of flowers, and a silver beverage cart stacked with china cups. It feels like a fancy department store, and we stand there, two parents, a girl, a cat, and a ghost, all of us so obviously, thoroughly, out of place.

"*Bienvenue,*" says the woman at the front desk, her eyes flicking from us to our luggage to the black cat in his carrier.

"Hello," says Mom cheerfully, and the clerk switches to English.

"Welcome to the Hotel Valeur. Have you stayed with us before?"

"No," says Dad. "This is our first time in Paris."

"Oh?" The woman arches a dark eyebrow. "What brings you to our city?"

"We're here on business," says Dad, at the same time Mom answers, "We're filming a television show."

The clerk's mood changes, lips pursing in displeasure.

"Ah yes," she says, "you must be the . . . *ghost finders*." The way she says it makes my face get hot and my stomach turn.

Beside me, Jacob cracks his knuckles. "I see we have a skeptic in the house."

A month ago, he couldn't even fog a window. Now he's looking around for something he can break. His attention lands on the beverage cart. I shoot him a warning look, mouthing the word *no*.

Lara's voice echoes in my head.

Ghosts don't belong in the in-between, and they certainly don't belong on this *side of it.*

The longer he stays, the stronger he'll get.

"We're paranormal investigators," corrects Mom.

The desk clerk's nose crinkles. "I doubt you will find such things here," she says, her perfectly manicured nails clicking across her keyboard. "Paris is a place of art, and culture, and history."

"Well," starts Dad, "I'm a historian and—"

But Mom puts a hand on his shoulder, as if to say, *This isn't a fight worth having.*

The woman at the desk gives us our keys. In that moment, Jacob succeeds in nudging the beverage cart and sends a china cup skating toward the edge. I reach out, steadying the cup before it can fall.

"Bad ghost," I whisper.

"No fun," answers Jacob as we follow my parents upstairs.

Back in Scotland, people talked about ghosts the way you might talk about your weird aunt or that odd kid in your neighborhood. Something out of place, sure, but undeniably *there*. Edinburgh was haunted from its tip to its toes, its castle to its caves. Even the Lane's End, the cute little bed-and-breakfast where we stayed, had a resident ghost.

But here, in the Hotel Valeur, there are no dark corners, no ominous sounds.

The door to our room doesn't even groan when it swings open.

We're staying in a suite, with a bedroom on each side

and an elegant sitting room in between. Everything is crisp, clean, and new.

Jacob looks at me, aghast. "It's almost like you *want* it to be haunted."

"No," I shoot back. "It's just . . . strange that it's not."

Dad must have heard me because he says, "What does *Jacob* think about our new digs?"

I roll my eyes.

It comes in handy, having a ghost for a best friend. I can sneak him into the movies, I don't have to share my snacks, and I never really get lonely. Of course, when your BFF isn't bound by the laws of *corporeality*, you have to lay down some ground rules. No intentional scaring. No going through closed bedroom or bathroom doors. No disappearing in the middle of a fight.

But there are drawbacks. It's always awkward when you get caught "talking to yourself." But even that's not as awkward as Dad thinking Jacob is my imaginary friend— some kind of preteen coping mechanism.

"Jacob is worried he's the only ghost here."

He scowls. "Stop putting words in my mouth."

I set Grim free, and he promptly climbs on top of the

sofa and announces his displeasure. I'm pretty sure he's cursing us for his most recent confinement, but maybe he's just hungry.

Mom pours some kibble into a dish, Dad sets about unpacking, and I drop my stuff in the smaller of the two bedrooms. When I come back out, Mom has thrown open one of the windows and she's leaning out on the wrought-iron rail, drawing in a deep breath.

"What a beautiful evening," she says, ushering me over. The sun has gone down, and the sky is a mottle of pink, and purple, and orange. Paris stretches in every direction. The Rue de Rivoli below is still crowded, and from this height, I can see beyond the trees to a massive stretch of green.

"That," says Mom, "is the Tuileries. It's a *jardin*—a garden, if you will."

Past the garden is a large river Mom tells me is called the Seine, and beyond that, a wall of pale stone buildings, all of them grand, all of them pretty. But the longer I look at Paris, the more I wonder.

"Hey, Mom," I say. "Why are we here? This city doesn't seem that haunted."

Mom beams. "Don't let looks fool you, Cass. Paris is

brimming with ghost stories." She nods toward the garden. "Take the Tuileries, for instance, and the legend of Jean the Skinner."

"Don't ask," says Jacob, even as I take the bait.

"Who was he?"

"Well," Mom says in her conversational way, "about five hundred years ago, there was a queen named Catherine, and she had a henchman named Jean the Skinner."

"This story," says Jacob, "is definitely going to end well."

"Jean went around dispatching Catherine's enemies. But the problem was, as time went on, he learned too many of the queen's secrets. And so, to keep her royal business private, she eventually ordered his death, too. He was killed right there in the Tuileries. Only when they went back to collect his body the next day, it was gone." Mom splays her fingers, as if performing a magic trick. "His corpse was never found, and ever since, all throughout history, Jean has appeared to kings and queens, a portent of doom for the monarchs of France."

And with that, she turns back to the room.

Dad's sitting on the sofa, his show binder open on the coffee table. In a display of *almost* catlike behavior, Grim wanders over and scratches his whiskers on the corner of the binder.

The label printed on its front reads: THE INSPECTERS.

The Inspecters was the title of my parents' book, when it was just ink and paper, and not a TV show. The irony is that back when they decided to *write* about all things paranormal, *I* didn't have any firsthand experience yet. I hadn't crashed my bike over a bridge, hadn't fallen into an icy river, hadn't (almost) drowned, hadn't met Jacob, hadn't gained the ability to cross the Veil, and hadn't learned that I was a ghost hunter.

Jacob clears his throat, clearly uncomfortable with the term.

I shoot him a look. *Ghost . . . saver?*

He arches a brow. "Awfully high and mighty."

Salvager?

He frowns. "I'm not scrap parts."

Specialist?

He considers. "Hmm, better. But it lacks a certain style."

Anyway, I think pointedly, my parents had no clue. They still don't, but now their show means that I get to see new places and meet new people—both the living and the dead.

Mom opens the binder, flipping to the second tab, which reads:

THE INSPECTERS
EPISODE TWO
LOCATION: Paris, France

And there, below, the title of the episode:

"TUNNEL OF BONES"

"Well," says Jacob pointedly, "*that* sounds promising."

"Let's see what we've got," says Mom, turning to a map of the city. There are numbers spiraling out from the center of the map, counting up from first to twentieth.

"What are those for?" I ask.

"*Arrondissements,*" says Dad. He explains that *arrondissement* is a fancy French word for *neighborhood.*

I sit on the sofa beside Mom as she turns to the filming schedule.

THE CATACOMBS

THE JARDIN DU LUXEMBOURG

THE EIFFEL TOWER

THE PONT MARIE BRIDGE

THE CATHEDRAL OF NOTRE-DAME

The list goes on. I resist the urge to reach for the folder and study each and every location the way my parents clearly have. Instead, I want to hear *them* tell the stories, want to stand in the places and learn the tales the way the viewers of the show will.

"Oh, yeah," says Jacob sarcastically, "who wants to be prepared when you can just fling yourself into the unknown?"

Let me guess, I think, *you were the kind of kid who flipped to the back of the book and read the ending first.*

"No," mutters Jacob, and then, "I mean, only if it was scary . . . or sad . . . or I was worried about the— Look, it doesn't matter."

I suppress a smile.

"Cassidy," says Mom, "your father and I have been talking . . ."

Oh no. The last time Mom put on her "family meeting" voice, I found out my summer plans were being replaced by a TV show.

"We want you to be more involved," says Dad.

"Involved?" I ask. "How?" We already had a long talk, before the traveling started, about how I'm good with not being on camera. I've always been more comfortable behind it, taking—

"Photos," says Mom. "For the show."

"Think of it as a look behind the scenes," says Dad. "Bonus content. The network would love some added material and we thought it might be nice for you to help in a more hands-on way."

"And keep you out of trouble," adds Jacob, who's now perched on the back of the sofa.

Maybe he's right. Maybe this is just a ploy to keep me from wandering off and getting my life thread stolen by powerful ghosts, and avoid being charged with misdemeanors for defiling graveyards.

But I'm still flattered.

"I'd love to," I say, hugging my camera to my chest.

"Great," says Dad, rising to stretch. "We don't start filming until tomorrow. How about we go out for some fresh air? Perhaps a walk through the Tuileries?"

"Perfect," says Mom cheerfully. "Maybe we'll get a glimpse of good old Jean."

CHAPTER TWO

Calling the Tuileries a *garden* is like calling Hogwarts a *school*.

It's technically correct, but the word really doesn't do either one justice.

Twilight is quickly giving way to night as we enter the park. The sandy path is as wide as a road, flanked by rows of trees that arch overhead, blotting out what's left of the sunset. More paths branch off, framing wide green lawns, trimmed here and there with roses.

I feel like I've stepped into *Alice in Wonderland*.

I always thought that book was a little scary, and so is the garden. Maybe it's because everything is spookier at night. It's why people are afraid of the dark. What you *can't* see is always scarier than what you can. Your eyes play tricks on you, filling in the shadows, making shapes. But night isn't the only thing that makes the garden creepy.

With every step, the Veil gets a little heavier, the murmur of ghosts a little louder.

Maybe Paris *is* more haunted than I thought.

Mom loops her arm through Dad's. "What a magnificent place," she muses, leaning her head against his shoulder.

"The Tuileries have quite a history," says Dad, putting on his teacher voice. "They were created in the sixteenth century as royal gardens for the palace."

At the far end of the Tuileries, beyond a section of roses that would rival the Queen of Hearts's, is the largest building I've ever seen. It's as wide as the *jardin* itself and shaped like a U, arms wrapping the end of the park in a giant stone hug.

"What is *that*?" I ask.

"That would be the palace," explains Dad. "Or the latest version of it. The original burned down in 1871."

As we get closer, I see something rising from the palace's courtyard—a glowing glass pyramid. Dad explains that these days, the palace houses a museum called the Louvre.

I frown at the pyramid. "It doesn't seem big enough to be a museum."

Dad laughs. "That's because the museum is *beneath* it," he says. "And around it. The pyramid is only the entrance."

"A reminder," says Mom, "that there's always more than meets the eye—"

She's cut off by a scream.

It pierces the air, and Jacob and I both jump. The sound is high and faint, and for a moment I think it's coming through the Veil. But then I realize the shouts are sounds of happiness. We walk past another wall of trees and find a *carnival*. Complete with Ferris wheels, small roller coasters, tented games, and food stalls.

My heart flutters at the sight of it all, and I'm already moving toward the colorful rides when a breeze blows through, carrying the scents of sugar and pastry dough. I stop short and turn, searching for the source of the heavenly smell, and see a stall advertising CRÊPES.

"What's a cre-ep?" I ask, sounding out the word.

Dad chuckles. "It's pronounced 'creh-p,'" he explains. "And it's like a thin pancake, covered in butter and sugar, or chocolate, or fruit, and folded into a cone."

"Sounds intriguing," I say.

"Sounds *amazing*," says Jacob.

Mom produces a few silver and gold coins. "It would be a travesty to come to France without trying one," she says as we join the back of the line. When we reach the counter, I watch as a man spreads batter paper-thin over the surface of a skillet.

He asks a question in French and stares at me, waiting for an answer.

"*Chocolat*," answers Dad, and I don't have to know French to understand *that*.

The man flips the crêpe and spreads a ladleful of chocolate over the entire surface before folding the delicate pancake in half, and then in quarters, and sliding it into a paper cone.

Dad pays, and Mom takes the crêpe. We head for the white tables and chairs scattered along the path and sit, bathed in carnival lights.

"Here, dear daughter," says Mom, offering me the crêpe. "Educate yourself."

I take a bite, and my mouth fills with the hot, sweet pancake, the rich chocolate spread. It is simple and wonderful. As we sit, passing the crêpe back and forth, Dad stealing

22

giant bites and Mom wiping a smudge of chocolate from her nose and Jacob watching the turn of the Ferris wheel with his wide blue eyes, I almost forget why we're here. I snap a photo of my parents, the carnival at their backs, and imagine that we're just a family on vacation.

But then I feel the tap on my shoulder, the press of the Veil against my back, and my attention drifts toward the shadowy part of the park. It calls to me. I used to think it was just curiosity that drew me toward the in-between. But now I know it's something else.

Purpose.

Jacob's eyes flit toward me. "No," he says, even as I get to my feet.

"Everything okay?" asks Mom.

"Yeah," I say, "I need to use the bathroom."

"No, you don't," whispers Jacob.

"I saw one, just past the food stalls," says Mom, pointing.

"Cassidy," whines Jacob.

"I'll be right back," I tell my parents.

I'm already moving away when Dad calls out, warning me not to wander off.

"I won't," I call back.

Dad shoots me a stern look. I'm still winning back their trust after the whole getting-trapped-in-the-Veil-by-a-ghost-and-having-to-fight-to-steal-my-life-back-by-hiding-in-an-open-grave thing (or, as *my parents* think of it, the afternoon I disappeared without permission and was found several hours later after breaking into a grave-yard).

Po-tay-to, po-tah-to.

I slip past the stalls and veer right, off the main path.

"Where are we going?" demands Jacob.

"To see if Jean the Skinner's still here."

"You've got to be joking."

But I'm not. I check my back pocket for my mirror pendant. It was a parting gift from Lara.

She would be furious at me for keeping the pendant in my pocket instead of out around my neck. She says people like us aren't only hunters; we're beacons for specters and spirits. Mirrors work on *all* ghosts, including Jacob, which is why I don't wear the pendant. Lara would probably say that's why I should.

Needless to say, she doesn't approve of Jacob.

"Lara doesn't approve of anything," he quips.

They don't get along—call it a difference of opinion.

"Her opinion," he snaps, "is that I don't belong here."

"Well, technically you *don't*," I whisper, wrapping the necklace around my wrist. "Now, let's go find Jean."

Jacob scowls, the air around him rippling ever so slightly with his displeasure. "We were having such a nice night."

"Come on," I say, closing my fingers over the mirror charm. "Aren't you curious?"

"Actually, no," he says, crossing his arms as I reach for the Veil. "I'm really not. I'm perfectly content to never find out if—"

I don't hear the rest. I pull the curtain aside and step through, and the world around me—

Vanishes.

The carnival lights, the crowds, the sounds and smells of the summer night. Gone. For a second, I'm falling. Plunging down into icy water, the shock of cold in my lungs. And then I'm back on my feet.

I've never gotten used to that part.

I don't think I ever will.

I straighten and let out a shaky breath as the world settles around me again, stranger, paler.

This is the Veil.

The in-between.

It's quiet and dark, full night. No carnival, no crowds, and thanks to the deep shadows and the tendrils of fog rolling across the lawns, I can barely see.

Jacob appears beside me a second later, obviously sulking.

"You didn't have to come," I say.

His foot scuffs the grass. "Whatever."

I smile. Rule number twenty-one of friendship: Friends don't leave friends in the Veil.

Jacob looks different here, fleshed out and colored in, and I can't see through him anymore. Meanwhile *I'm* less solid than I was before, washed out and gray, with one glaring exception: the ribbon of light shining through my rib cage.

Not just a ribbon, but a life.

My life.

It glows with a pale blue-white light, and if I were to

reach into my chest and pull it out, like some kind of grue-some show-and-tell, you'd see it's not perfect anymore. There's a seam, a thin crack, where it got torn in two. I put it back together, and it seems to be working well enough, but I have no desire to test how much damage a lifeline can take.

"Oh well," says Jacob, craning his head, "looks like no one's here. We better go."

I'm as nervous as he is, but I hold my ground. Someone *is* here. They have to be here. That's the thing about the Veil: It only exists where there's a ghost. It's like a stage where spirits act out their final hours, whatever happened that won't let them move on.

My hands go to the camera around my neck, and the mirror pendant wrapped around my wrist chimes faintly as metal hits metal. The sound echoes strangely in the dark.

As my eyes adjust, I realize that buildings outside the park are gone, erased either by time—if they haven't been built yet—or simply by the boundaries of this particular in-between, whoever it belongs to.

The question is, whose life—or, rather, death—are we in?

The night sky is getting brighter, tinged with a faint orange glow.

"Um, Cass," says Jacob, looking over my shoulder.

I turn and stop, my eyes widening in surprise.

There's no Jean the Skinner, but there *is* a palace.

And it's on fire.

CHAPTER THREE

The fog isn't fog at all, but *smoke*.

The wind picks up, and the fire quickens, the air darkening with soot. I can hear shouting, and carriages rattling over stone, and through the smoke I see a huddle of figures on the lawn, faces turned up toward the blaze.

I step closer, lift the camera's viewfinder to my eye, and take a picture.

"Cass . . ." says Jacob, but he sounds far away, and when I turn to look for him, all I see is smoke.

"Jacob?" I call out, coughing as the smoke tickles my throat, creeps into my lungs. "Where are—"

A shape crashes into me. I stumble back into the grass, and the man drops the bucket he was hauling. It topples onto the ground, spilling something black and viscous. I know instantly that this is *his* place in the Veil. The other ghosts are just set pieces, puppets, but this man's eyes, as they fall on me, are haunted.

I scramble to my feet, already holding up the mirror pendant, ready to send him on—

But there's no necklace wrapped around my wrist, no mirror hanging in the air.

I look down, scouring the ground where I fell, and see the necklace shining in the grass, where it must have slipped off. But before I can reach it, the ghost grabs me by the collar and pushes me back against a tree. I try to twist free, but even though he's a ghost and I'm not, the Veil levels the playing field.

"Jacob!" I shout. The man's grip tightens as he spews at me in French, the words a mystery but the tone clear and cruel. And then he trails off, his eyes dropping to the camera at my chest.

No, not the camera, I realize with horror. The thread. The blue-white glow of my life. He grabs for it, and I squirm, desperate to get away from the reaching fingers—

"Hey!" shouts a familiar voice, and the ghost looks sideways just as Jacob swings the bucket at his head.

The man staggers, black tar dripping down his face, and I gasp, dropping to the ground. The instant I'm free,

I lunge for the fallen necklace as the ghost takes one half-blinded step toward me. I grab the necklace and scramble up, holding the pendant out in front of me like a shield.

The ghost comes to a halt, his attention caught on the little round surface of the mirror.

A mirror, explained Lara, to reflect the truth. To show the spirit what they are.

The mirror traps the ghost, but the words, the spell, the incantation send them on. I didn't know there *were* words until a week ago, didn't know about the power of mirrors, or lifelines. But as I stand here now, facing the specter, my mind goes blank.

I can't remember the words.

Panic rushes through me as I grasp for them, find nothing.

And then Jacob leans in and whispers in my ear.

"Watch and listen," he prompts.

And just like that, I remember.

I swallow, finding my voice.

"Watch and listen," I order the ghost. "See and know. This is what you are."

The whole Veil ripples around us, and the ghost thins until I can see through him, see the dark thread coiled inside his chest. Lightless, lifeless.

I reach out and take hold of his thread, the last thing binding him here, to this world. It feels cold and dry under my fingers, like dead leaves in the fall. As I pull the cord from his chest, it crumbles in my palm. Vanishes in a plume of smoke.

And then, so does the ghost.

He dissolves, ash and then air. There and then gone.

Jacob shudders a little in discomfort, but for me, it's like coming up for air. In those seconds, right after the ghost moves on, I feel . . . right.

What you feel, said Lara, *is called a* purpose.

The palace continues to burn, and I sway on my feet, dizzy, the effect of the Veil catching up with me.

A warning that I've stayed too long.

"Come on." Jacob takes my hand and pulls me back through the Veil. I shiver as the curtain brushes my skin. For an instant, the cold floods my lungs again, the water pulling me down—and then we're back on solid ground.

The park is bright and loud, filled with carnival lights and tourists and evening warmth. Jacob is faded again, vaguely see-through, and I'm solid, the bright coil of my life hidden safely beneath flesh and bone.

"Thanks," I say, shaking off the chill.

"We're a team," says Jacob, holding up his hand. "Ghost five."

He makes a smacking sound as I bring my palm against his. But this time, I swear I feel a faint pressure, like steam, before my hand goes through. I look at Jacob's face, wondering if he feels it, too, but he's already turning away.

"There you are!" says Mom, holding out the last bite of crêpe as I return to the table. "I had to shield this from your father. Nearly lost a finger."

"Sorry," I say, "the line was long."

(I don't like lying to my parents, but I tried telling them the truth, after the whole incident in the graveyard, and they didn't believe me. So maybe that makes this lie a little smaller.)

"Yeah," says Jacob, "keep telling yourself that."

Dad rises, brushing off his hands. "Well, darling family,"

he says, wrapping an arm around my shoulders. "We better head back."

The darkness is heavy now, and the Veil is still pressing against me, calling me back. But as we make our way through the Tuileries, I'm careful to stick to the path, and stay in the light.

CHAPTER FOUR

The next morning, our local guide is waiting for us in the hotel's *salon* (the dining room).

She's tall and slim, in a green blouse and a cream-colored skirt. She has high cheekbones in a heart-shaped face and dark hair pulled up in a complicated bun. She's younger than I expected, maybe in her twenties.

"You must be Madame Deschamp," says Mom, holding out her hand.

"Please," says the woman in a silky voice, "call me Pauline."

Her French accent makes everything sound musical. It's funny—I used to think the same thing about Scottish accents. But now I realize the accents are like two kinds of music, as different as a ballad and a lullaby.

Dad says something in French, and Mom laughs, and suddenly I feel left out, like they've told a joke I don't get.

"You speak well," says Pauline, and Dad blushes.

"I studied in college," he says, "but I'm afraid I'm rusty."

"Pauline," says Mom, "this is our daughter, Cassidy."

Jacob sticks his hands in his pockets and mumbles, "Don't bother introducing *me*."

"*Enchantée*," says Pauline, turning toward me. Her gaze is steady, searching. "*Parlez-vous français?*"

It's my turn to blush now. "No, sorry. Just English."

I did take Italian in school last year, but I was really, *really* bad at it, and I don't think being able to ask where the library is in another language will help me here. The only French I've managed to pick up is *s'il vous plaît*, which means *please*, and *merci*, which means *thank you*.

A server drifts over, and Pauline exchanges a few words in rapid French before urging us to sit. "We're so grateful to have you as our guide," says Dad.

"Yes," Pauline says slowly, "it should be . . . interesting." She smooths her blouse as if brushing away crumbs.

"Tell me," says Mom, "do you believe in ghosts?"

Pauline's expression goes stiff.

"*No,*" she says, the word quick and crisp, like slamming a door on something you don't want to see. "I'm sorry.

That was rude. I will explain: I am an emissary, here on behalf of the French Ministry of Culture. I spend most of my time with dignitaries and documentarians. This is not an *ordinary* assignment for me, but I am Parisian. I have lived here all my life. I will take you where you wish to go. I will help in any way I can. But I cannot say that I believe."

"That's fine," says Dad. "I'm here for the history. My wife is the believer."

Pauline looks at me.

"And you, Cassidy?" she asks. "Do *you* believe?"

Jacob arches a brow in my direction. "Yes, do tell me," he says. "What is your stance on ghosts?"

I smile, and nod at Pauline. "It's hard to believe in ghosts, until you see one, and then it's hard *not* to."

A small crinkle appears, right between Pauline's perfect eyebrows. "Perhaps."

The server returns with three of the smallest cups I've ever seen (seriously, they look like they're from the tea party set I had when I was five) full of dark coffee.

"And for the mademoiselle," he says, handing me a mug of hot chocolate dusted with cocoa.

He also sets down a basketful of pastries. I recognize the crescent shape of a croissant, but the spiral and the rectangle are a mystery. I reach for the rectangle and bite into it, only to discover that the center is *filled with chocolate.*

Paris has just gone up a notch in my book.

"Pain au chocolat," explains Mom as I take another bite. Between the hot cocoa, which is rich and thick, and the pastry, I can feel my pupils dilating. Back home, I'm not even allowed to eat sugar cereal.

Jacob sighs. "I miss sugar."

More for me. Buttery flakes rain down on the table as I take another bite.

Pauline's gaze flicks up toward the salon entrance and her expression warms. "Ah, the crew has arrived. Anton!" she says, rising to her feet. "Annette."

They turn out to be a pair of siblings. They have the same brown hair, pointed chins, and gray-blue eyes. But otherwise, they look like shadows at different times of day—Anton is as tall and thin as a skeleton, while Annette is short and square.

Pauline kisses each of them twice, once on each cheek, then turns to my parents.

"If you are ready, we should leave. We will start with the Catacombs."

"Yes," says Mom, brushing sugar from her lap. "The ghosts of Paris await."

"What's a catacomb?" I ask as we step outside.

"It's a kind of graveyard," says Dad.

"Like Greyfriars?" I ask, thinking of the hilly cemetery nestled in the heart of Edinburgh.

"Not exactly," he says. "It's—"

"Don't ruin the surprise," says Mom, which makes me intensely nervous. Mom's idea of a surprise has always been less *Happy birthday* and more *Look at this vaguely nightmarish thing I found in the backyard.* "Just wait, Cass," she says. "The Paris Catacombs are one of the most famous places in the world."

"At least she didn't say most *haunted*," muses Jacob, right before Mom adds, "And *definitely* one of the most haunted."

Jacob sighs. "Of course."

We take the Metro across the city and get off at a stop called Denfert-Rochereau.

Outside, I notice a placard on a building's stone wall that says *14ᵉ*: the number of the neighborhood we're in. As we walk, I keep my eyes peeled for a graveyard, but all I see are normal buildings. And yet I know we're getting closer because I can feel the *tap-tap-tap* of ghosts getting louder with every step.

The Veil ripples around me, and the beat shifts from my chest to my feet, a heavy bass drumming through the street. Haunted places don't just call to me. They drag me in like a fish on a line. There's no hook, only a thread, wisp-thin but strong as wire, connecting me to the other side.

My parents, Pauline, and the crew come to an abrupt stop in front of a small green hut. It's plain and inconspicuous, more like a newspaper stand than a place for the dead. In fact, it doesn't look large enough to hold more than one or two coffins. At first I think we must be in the wrong place, but then I see the copper plaque nailed to the painted wood.

ENTRÉE DES CATACOMBES.

"Huh," I say. "I thought the Catacombs would be ... bigger."

"Oh, they are," says Dad, pulling out one of his guidebooks. He shows me a map of Paris, and then turns the page in front of it. A filmy sheet of paper settles over the map, its translucent surface traced with red lines.

Slowly, I realize what I'm looking at. I also realize why I felt so weird as we walked.

The Catacombs aren't in this little green hut.

They're under our feet. And judging by the map in Dad's hand, they're under a *lot* of people's feet. The Catacombs are a coil of tunnels twisting back and forth on themselves beneath the city.

We approach the door, but a sign on the wall announces that the Catacombs are closed.

"Oh, too bad," says Jacob. "We'll just have to come back another time . . ." He trails off as a man in a security uniform appears, unlocking the entrance to the little green shack and ushering us through.

Inside, there's a pair of turnstiles, like the beginning of a roller-coaster ride.

We pass through and find ourselves at the top of a spiral staircase wide enough for only one person at a time.

It plunges down out of sight. The tunnels below seem to exhale, sending up a draft of cool, stale air, along with a wave of anger, and fear, and restless loss.

"Nope," says Jacob, shaking his head.

This is a bad place, and we can both feel it.

I hesitate as the Veil tightens its grip, calling me down even as something deep in my bones tells me to stay put, or even better, to run.

Mom looks back over her shoulder. "Cass? You okay?"

"Just tell them you're too scared," says Jacob.

But I'm not, I think. I *am* scared, but there's a difference between being scared to do something and being *too* scared to do it. *Plus*, I think, clutching my camera, *I have a job to do*. And I don't even mean ghost-hunting. My parents asked for my help. I don't want to let them down.

And so I propel myself forward and take the first step.

"Everything about this is terrible," says Jacob as we descend, down, down, down into the tunnels under Paris.

CHAPTER FIVE

I used to have this one bad dream.

I was trapped in a room, deep under the earth. The room was glass, so I could see the dirt on every side, pressing against the walls.

The dream was always the same. First I would get bored, and then I would get nervous, and then, at last, I would get scared. Sometimes I would bang on the walls, and sometimes I would sit perfectly still, but every time, no matter what I did, a crack would form in the glass.

The crack would spread and spread, up the walls and overhead, until bits of dirt came through and then, just as the ceiling shattered, I'd wake up.

I haven't thought of that dream in years.

But I think about it now.

The spiral stairs are a tight coil, so we can't see more than a full turn at a time, and they just keep going, and going, and going.

"How far down are the Catacombs?" I ask, fighting to keep the fear out of my voice.

"About five stories," says Dad, and I try not to think about the fact that the Hotel Valeur is only four stories tall.

"Why would you put a graveyard underground?" I ask.

"The Catacombs weren't always used as a graveyard," explains Dad. "Before they became an ossuary, the tunnels were simply stone quarries that ran beneath the growing city."

"What's an ossuary?" I ask.

"It's a place where the bones of the dead are stored."

Jacob and I exchange a look. "What happened to the rest of them?"

Mom chuckles. It doesn't make me feel any better.

"The bodies in the Catacombs were transferred here from other graves," explains Pauline.

Transferred.

Meaning *dug up*.

"Oh, I do not like this," says Jacob. "I do not like this *at all*."

"Today," says Dad, "the Catacombs are home to more than six million bodies."

44

I nearly trip on the steps. I must have heard him wrong.

"That's three times the *living* population of Paris," adds Mom cheerfully.

I feel a little queasy. Jacob glowers at me as if to say, *This is your fault.*

We finally reach the bottom of the stairs, and the Veil washes up around me like a tide, dragging at my limbs. I push back, trying to keep my footing as Jacob draws closer.

"We are *not* crossing here," he says, all the humor gone from his voice. "Do you hear me, Cass? We are *not. Crossing. Here.*"

He doesn't have to tell me.

I have no desire to find out what's on the other side of this particular Veil.

Especially when I see what's ahead of us.

I'd been hoping for a large space, like one of those giant caves with stalactites—stalagmites? I can never remember which is which—but instead there is only a tunnel.

The ground is a mix of rough stone and packed dirt, and the walls look dug by hand. Here and there, water drips from the low ceiling. Electric lights have been spaced out, casting dim yellow pools among patches of shadow.

"Well, this is cozy," says Mom.

I swallow hard as we start walking. *The only way out is through*, I tell myself.

"Or, you know, back up those stairs," says Jacob.

Come on, I think. *Where's your sense of adventure?*

"I must have left it up on street level," he mutters.

Mom and Dad walk on ahead, narrating for the cameras. I glance over at Pauline, who's focused on where she's stepping, careful to avoid the shallow pools of water, the muddy dirt patches between stones.

I lean toward her and whisper, "I expected more bones."

"We haven't made it to the tombs yet," she explains, her voice echoing off the low ceiling. "These are only the galleries. Relics from the days when these tunnels served less grim purposes."

The tunnel twists and turns, sometimes wide enough for two people, and sometimes so narrow we have to walk single file. The Veil presses against my back like a hand, urging me forward.

"You know the only thing worse than a haunted place?" asks Jacob.

What?

"One you can't easily *leave*."

You don't know *it's haunted*, I think, sounding thoroughly unconvinced.

"How can it *not* be?" he counters. "Have you forgotten George Mackenzie?"

George Mackenzie was one of the ghosts in a cemetery back in Scotland. He didn't start haunting the graveyard until some vandals disturbed his bones.

That was *one man*.

But maybe the stories are wrong. Maybe he was already restless.

"And maybe they're all friendly ghosts down here," says Jacob, "just having a grand old time."

Mom pulls out a small box, its surface studded with lights. An EMF meter—a tool meant to register disturbances in the electromagnetic force. Also known as *ghosts*. She switches it on, but the meter only registers a muffled static as she lets it trail over the wall.

We reach the end of the galleries, and the tunnel opens into a chamber, the walls lined with glass cases, like in a

47

museum. The glass cases hold text and pictures, explaining how the Catacombs came to be. But the thing that catches my eye is the doorway on the other side.

A stone mantel looms over it, the words carved in bold French type.

ARRÊTE! C'EST ICI L'EMPIRE DE LA MORT.

"*Stop!*" recites Dad, his voice bouncing off the close stone walls. "*This here is the Empire of the Dead.*"

"Not ominous," mutters Jacob. "Not ominous at all."

"In the 1700s," continues Dad, addressing Annette's camera, "Paris had a problem. The dead outnumbered the living, and the living had no place to put them. The graveyards were overflowing, sometimes literally, and something had to be done. And so the conversion of the Catacombs began."

"It would take two whole years," says Mom, "to move the bodies of the dead. Imagine, a nightly procession of corpse-filled wagons rattling through the streets, as six million dead were ferried from their resting places into the tunnels beneath Paris."

It's so weird, watching them like this. The way they transform in front of the camera. They don't become different *people*, they just become sharper, louder, more colorful. The same song with the volume turned up. Dad, the image of a scholar. Mom, the picture of a dreamer. Together, "the Inspecters" look larger than life. I snap a photo of them being filmed as Dad goes on.

"For decades," he says, "the bones of the dead littered these tunnel floors, the remains piled haphazardly throughout the vast tomb. It wasn't until an engineer by the name of Louis-Étienne Héricart decided to convert the grave into a place for visitors that the real transformation began and the Empire of the Dead was formed."

Mom gestures, like a showman pulling back a curtain. "Shall we go in?"

"I think I'll wait here," says Jacob, suddenly fascinated by the glass cases.

Suit yourself, I think.

I follow the crew forward without looking back. And even though I can't *hear* Jacob's steps, I know he's there, on my heels, close as a shadow as we step through into a world of bones.

CHAPTER SIX

The bones are *everywhere*.

They line the dirt walls, a sea of skeletons rising almost to the ceiling. They form patterns, rippling designs—a wave of skulls set on a backdrop of femurs, the morbid decorations stacked as high as I can see. Empty eye sockets stare out, and jaws hang open. Some of the bones are broken, crumbling, and others look startlingly fresh. If you squint hard enough, the pieces disappear, and you're left with a pattern of wavering grays that could be stone instead of bone.

Our shadows dance on the walls, and I take photo after photo, knowing the camera will only capture what's here, only see the real. But right now, the real is strange enough. Strange, and chilling, and almost—beautiful.

"And horrifying," says Jacob. "Don't forget horrifying."

We round a corner, and as if on cue, the EMF meter in

Mom's hand erupts from static into a high-pitched whine that echoes through the tunnels like a scream.

Mom jumps, and quickly switches the unit back off.

"Well," she says, her voice a little shaky. "I think that says enough."

I shiver, unsettled.

Even Pauline is looking tense.

"Gee, what could possibly be making her nervous?" muses Jacob. "Is it the fact we're five stories underground? Or that this tunnel is roughly the size of a coffin? Or could it be the fact we're surrounded by *six million bodies*?"

Six million—it's a number so big it doesn't seem real.

Two hundred and seventy—that's a better number. Still a lot, but countable. Two hundred and seventy is the number of bones you have when you're born. Some of them fuse together as you grow, so by the time you're an adult, you have two hundred and six (thanks, Science class).

So, if the Catacombs are home to more than six million bodies, how many bones?

Six million times two hundred and six is—a lot. Too many to capture in a photo. But picture this: It's enough bones to stack five feet high throughout every one of the tunnels under Paris. An Empire of the Dead as large as the city, the bodies unmarked and unknown.

Jacob begins to sing, and it takes me a solid thirty seconds to realize what he's singing.

"... *the foot bone's connected to the leg bone, the leg bone's connected to the knee bone* ..."

"Are you serious?" I whisper.

He throws up his hands. "Just trying to have a sense of humor about this."

We wind our way through the tunnels, the locked iron gates converting the maze around us into a clear path. I wonder how easy it would be to get lost without those doors.

"Do you see this line overhead?" asks Dad, the question directed at the cameras as much as us.

I stare up and see a thick black mark painted on the ceiling.

"Back before they installed lights and gates, that was the only way to keep people from getting lost."

I try to imagine coming down here before there was electricity, armed with just lanterns or candles. I shudder.

The only thing that would make this place creepier would be being down here in the dark.

Mom turns to the camera.

"Over the years," she says, "more than a few travelers have wandered down into these tunnels, to seek shelter, perhaps, or simply to explore, only to get lost amid the many halls. Many never found their way out again. At least, not while they were still alive."

The Veil leans heavy on my shoulders, urging me to cross over, but I manage to hold my ground. I feel like I'm the glass box in my dream, the world pressing in from every side. But I don't crack.

There's no question Jacob is getting stronger.

But maybe I am, too.

"Over here," calls Dad, his voice echoing. *Here, here, here . . .*

The bone walls are interrupted every so often by stone plaques, their surfaces carved with quotes about life and death. Dad stops in front of one, and Pauline and I hang back so our shadows don't cross into the camera shot.

I glance sideways, and nearly jump out of my skin when

a skull stares back, its empty sockets at eye level. Before I can think, I'm reaching out to touch the bleached white bone and—

All at once the Veil bristles, rising to my fingertips. As it does, I hear the muffled sound of voices beyond: sad, and lonely, and lost. Someone is calling out, and I can almost, *almost* hear the words. I lean closer.

"Hello?" calls a voice from the shadows, sounding scared.

I look around, but no one else seems to hear it. My parents walk on, and Pauline looks straight ahead.

"Cassidy," hisses Jacob. "Don't."

My hand falls away, but I can still feel the Veil, sliding through my fingers like silk.

". . . s'il vous plaît . . ." comes another voice from the shadows, this one speaking French, the words thin and high and faint.

". . . no one is coming . . ." murmurs a third. And then a fourth voice—

"HELP!"

The shout is so sudden and loud that I scramble backward. My heel catches a bit of rock on the ground and

I stumble, unsteady. I reach out to catch myself, but this time, when my hand hits the wall, it keeps going, as if the surface is made of cloth instead of bone.

No, no, no, I think as the Veil parts beneath my fingers, and I fall down and through.

A short, sharp drop.

A shock of cold.

The taste of the river in my throat.

And then I'm on my hands and knees on the hard stone floor.

Pain scrapes across my palms, and my camera swings from the strap around my neck.

The tunnel is dark, and I blink my eyes rapidly, willing them to adjust. The only light I can see is the one coming from my own chest. The blue-white glow shines brightly, but only as far as my shirt. Not exactly a human flashlight. More like a human firefly.

I get to my feet, pulling the mirror from my back pocket.

"Jacob?" I whisper, but there's no answer.

As my eyes adjust, I realize there's another light, low and red, coming from around the corner. It reminds me of the light I use in my darkroom back home when I'm developing film.

I start toward it, and then I hear a small sound, like pebbles moving or feet shuffling over dirt, and the red light shrinks away.

"Hello?" I call, walking faster. But by the time I round the corner, the crimson light is gone, replaced by an old-fashioned lantern sitting on the ground. It throws off an unsteady yellow glow and casts shadows on the surrounding skulls, so it looks like they're grinning. Scowling. Shocked.

I realize then how quiet the tunnel is, how empty.

I heard the ghosts, didn't I? So where are they now?

Something moves behind me in the dark. I can feel it. My hand tightens on the pendant, and I'm working up the nerve to turn around when I hear the voice.

"Cassidy."

Jacob. I sag with relief and I turn, only to find his face sharp, angry.

"I thought we agreed not to do this," he says, arms folded tight across his chest.

"I didn't want to," I say. "I swear."

"Whatever," he says, "let's just go before something—"

A pebble skitters across the stone floor behind us.

"Did you hear that?" I ask.

"Could be the bones settling," he says, "or the wind."

But there's no wind down here, and we both know it wasn't the bones, especially when the next sound is the crunch of feet. Someone else is here. I start forward, but Jacob catches my hand.

"We have no map," he warns me.

He's right. Space is space. A step in the Veil is a step on the other side. If we wander too far away from my parents and the crew, I could end up lost in the real world, too. Trapped in this maze.

And then a playful young voice, somewhere in the distance, calls out in French.

"Un . . . deux . . . trois . . ."

"Nope," says Jacob. He's already pulling me backward, already reaching for the curtain.

"Wait," I say, trying to twist free as the voice calls again. But Jacob tightens his grip.

"Look," he says. "I get it. You can't help yourself. It's your nature. Your purpose, whatever. You have to look

57

under the bed. Open the closet. Peek behind the curtain. But have a little common sense, Cass. We are fifty feet underground, surrounded by bones with only a lantern for light, and I'm officially invoking rule twenty-one of friendship, and we are leaving right now, together."

He's right. I sigh, and nod. "Okay. Let's go."

Jacob exhales with relief, and grabs the curtain. The Veil ripples and parts, and I follow him through. But at the last second, before the Veil is swept away, I look back, into the tunnel, and I swear I see a shadow moving along the wall, its edges glowing red.

But then the Veil is gone, and I'm falling, ice water in my lungs before the world shutters back into focus, solid again, the lights bright. I hear the sounds of the camera crew packing up, and Pauline's high heels clicking on the rock floor, and my parents' voices moving toward me.

I'm on my knees on the grimy stones, but I hurriedly bring the camera's viewfinder to my eye. I snap a photo— an arch of skulls around a gravestone—the second before Mom rounds the corner.

"Cassidy," she says, exasperated. "I found her!" she calls back over her shoulder.

I manage a weak smile. "I was just taking some pictures," I say, my voice a little shaky, my hands and knees slick with dirt. "For the show."

"Too close, Cass," says Jacob. He leans moodily back against the wall—or at least he starts to. At the first brush of bone, he jumps away, shuddering in disgust.

Mom studies me for a moment, then nods. "I admire your dedication, dear daughter," she says, patting my hair, "but next time, stay where we can see you?"

"I'll try," I say as she kisses my head and pulls me to my feet.

As I follow her down the tunnel, I can't help but look back into the darkness, half expecting to see the red light dancing along the wall. But all I see is darkness, shadows falling over bones.

PART TWO

MISCHIEF MAKER

CHAPTER SEVEN

Do you ever feel like you're being followed?

That prickle on the back of your neck that tells you someone is watching?

I can't shake that feeling as we reach the top of the stairs, trading the tunnels for the Paris streets. As we walk, I keep glancing back over my shoulder, sure that I'll see something, someone, and every time I look, I feel like I've just missed them. My eyes start playing tricks on me, until every shadow looks like it's moving. Every streak of sunlight has a shape.

I try to tell myself it's nothing. Just the residual creeps, clinging like cobwebs.

It's lunchtime, and we snag a table at a sidewalk café. All of us, I think, are grateful for the fresh air. Mom and Dad discuss the next filming location—the Jardin du Luxembourg—and I order something called a croque monsieur, which turns out to be like a fancy grilled cheese with ham. As I eat, the warm sandwich helps dispel the last of the Catacombs' chill. But my attention keeps drifting down to the sidewalk, remembering the city of the dead under my feet. I wonder how many people cross these streets and never realize they're walking over bones.

"Morbid much?" calls Jacob over his shoulder.

He's standing in the sun, the light shining through him as he studies a rock on the curb, readying to kick it.

And then, out of nowhere, I shiver.

It's like someone put a cold hand on the back of my neck. It's all I can do not to yelp in surprise. A sharp breath hisses through my teeth.

Mom glances toward me, but before she can ask what's wrong, there's a ripping sound overhead. The edge of the café's awning tears free.

"Cassidy, look out!" shouts Jacob.

One of the metal hooks in the corner of the awning sweeps down toward our table, shattering the pitcher of water right in front of my seat.

I jump back just in time, avoiding all of the glass and most of the water.

Mom and Dad gasp, and Pauline's on her feet, one hand clutching the front of her blouse in surprise. Anton and Annette shake their heads and examine the broken awning, exchanging a flurry of French.

A waiter rushes out, full of apologies as he sweeps up the damage. He moves us to another table, and everyone tries to shake off the strangeness of the incident.

Mom keeps fussing over me, checking me for cuts. I assure her I'm okay, even though I'm feeling a little dizzy. I look back at our old table. It could have been nothing. A faulty screw in the awning. An old piece of cloth. Bad luck. But what about the rush of cold I felt, right before the awning broke? What was that? A warning?

"Do you think you're becoming psychic now?" asks Jacob.

Even though I'm 90 percent sure that's not in the in-betweener job description, I text Lara under the table.

Me:
Hey

Me:
Do people like us have any other powers?

A few moments later, Lara texts back.

Lara:
Some are intuitive. The more time they spend in the in-between, the stronger their spectral senses get.

Lara:
Why do you ask?

I hesitate before writing back.

Me:
Just curious. ☺

Lara:

Jacob looks over my shoulder. "Ha!" he says. "It looks just like her."

I have to hand it to the French: They really love dessert.

As we walk to the next location, we pass: shops devoted to chocolate; four window displays of small cakes as intricate and detailed as sculptures; countless ice cream carts; and counter after counter filled with tiny, brightly colored cookie sandwiches called macarons, in flavors like rose, caramel, blackberry, and lavender.

Mom buys a box of macarons and offers me one the

buttery color of sunshine. I try to focus on the cookie instead of the shaky feeling in my stomach, the stutter step of my pulse, the nagging sense that something is wrong.

When I bite into the macaron, the outside crackles before giving way to soft cream and a bright burst of citrus.

"Like a natural," says Pauline. "Next you must try escargot."

Mom and Dad both laugh, which makes me nervous. When I start to ask, Mom pats my shoulder and says, "You don't want to know."

Dad leans in and whispers in my ear, "Snails."

I really hope he's joking.

"Here we are," says Mom. "The Luxembourg Gardens."

"You keep using that word," says Jacob. "I don't think it means what you think it means."

He's got a point. These *gardens* look like they were designed using complicated math.

Massive trees, their tops cut into parallel lines, lead like giant green walls to another huge palace. The packed-sand paths carve the lawns into geometric shapes, their edges trimmed with roses and dotted by statues. The grass is so short and so smooth, I can imagine someone down on their hands and knees, trimming it blade by blade with a tiny pair of scissors.

Mom veers left, ducking onto a wooded path, and we follow. The sand crackles beneath our shoes as we walk, and then Mom stops and lowers herself onto a bench.

"Do you want to hear a story?" she says, her voice soft and sweet and creepy.

And just like that, we all shuffle closer. Mom has always had that power over people, always been the kind of story-teller who makes her listeners lean in.

Even Pauline can't really hide her interest. Her hand drifts to her collar as she listens, the way it has a few times today. *A nervous tic*, I think. Though it's strange. After all, she said she's a skeptic—what does she have to be nervous about?

Anton has started filming, and when Mom speaks again, she's not just talking to us but to an invisible audience.

"One lovely evening in 1925, a gentleman sat on a bench here in the Jardin du Luxembourg"—she pauses to pat the seat beside her—"enjoying a book in the fine weather, when a man in a black coat came up and invited him to his home for a concert. The gentleman accepted, and followed the man in black back to his apartment, where he found a party in full swing, and passed the night with music and wine and excellent company."

Mom flashes a mischievous grin and sits forward. "In the early hours of the morning, the gentleman left, but shortly after, he realized he was missing his cigarette lighter and returned to collect it. But when he arrived, he found the place dark, the doors and windows boarded shut. It was a neighbor who told him that a musician had once lived there, but that he'd died more than twenty years before."

A little shudder runs through me, but this one is simple, the almost-pleasant chill that comes with a good ghost story. Not like what I felt earlier at the café.

"And yet, to this day," finishes Mom, "if you linger in the park as the sun goes down, you just might be approached by a man in a black coat, extending the same invitation. The only question is, will you accept?"

"Finally!" says Jacob. "A friendly ghost story."

As Mom rises from the bench, a cold breeze blows past.

This one feels like the cool air I felt at the café. I'm fighting back another shiver when sand crackles under feet on the path behind me. I twist around, catching something— *someone*—in the corner of my eye.

But when I look at the path head-on, no one's there.

"Did you—" I start, but Jacob has already moved ahead with the rest of the group. I let out an unsteady breath.

"Cass?" calls Dad. "You coming?"

I frown, then jog to catch up.

"If you keep glancing over your shoulder," says Jacob, "you're going to hurt your neck."

He starts walking backward beside me. "Here, I'll look for you." He shoves his hands in his pockets and squints into the distance. "You still think we're being followed?"

"I don't know," I say, shaking my head. "Something just feels . . . off. It has all day."

"Maybe Mercury is in retrograde."

I look at him. "What does *that* mean?"

"I have no idea," admits Jacob, turning back around, "but I've heard people say it when things go wrong."

I frown. "I don't think planets have anything to do with this."

Jacob shrugs, and we walk in silence toward our final location for the day.

The Eiffel Tower isn't exactly subtle.

You can see it halfway across Paris, a dark lace spire against the sky. Up close, it's massive. It looms like a giant steel beast over the city.

The park at the tower's base is brimming with people, all sprawled in the afternoon sun, and the mood is the opposite of spooky. Yet when my parents start filming, I swear the clouds slide in and a light breeze rustles Mom's hair and casts a shadow on Dad's face.

They bring the atmosphere with them.

"The Eiffel Tower," says Dad as Anton films him. "One of the most famous architectural feats and iconic tourist attractions in the world. A marker of history."

Mom picks up, her voice smooth. "And story." She glances over her shoulder at the tower before continuing. "Back at the start of the twentieth century, a young American fell in love with a French girl, and after courting

71

her, he took her up the tower to propose. But when he drew out the ring, she was so surprised that she leaped back, slipped over the edge, and fell . . ."

I swallow, my skin humming with nervous energy. Maybe it's just the near miss at the café, but the Eiffel Tower suddenly looks like an accident waiting to happen.

"There are a dozen stories just like that," says Dad, sounding skeptical. "Perhaps they're simply urban legends."

"Or perhaps one of them is true," counters Mom. "Visitors claim to have seen a young woman, perched on the darkened rail, still grinning like a bride."

A small movement catches the corner of my eye.

It's Pauline. As Mom and Dad tell the story, her hand drifts up to her collar again. As I watch, she draws something out from beneath her blouse. It's a silver necklace, a pendant swinging from the end. My heart lurches, and I think of the mirror in my back pocket, ready to dispel any restless spirits.

But then her pendant catches the light, and I see it's not a mirror, but an ordinary bit of jewelry, a silver disc worn smooth from use. As I watch, she rubs her thumb over it, her lips moving as she whispers something to herself.

"What is that?" I ask, and she shows me the talisman. Most of the details have been worn away, but I can just make out the lines of an eye.

"It's an old symbol," she says, "meant to ward off evil."

"I thought you didn't believe in this kind of stuff."

"I don't," she answers quickly, waving her hand. "Just a bit of superstition." I'm not sure I believe her.

"Well," says Mom, coming over to us and clapping her hands. "Shall we go up?"

I swallow. "Up?" I echo, studying the tower.

Confession: I don't love heights. I wouldn't go so far as to say I'm *afraid* of them, but I'll never be the girl standing on the ledge, arms spread wide, like that moment in Harry Potter when Harry rides a hippogriff for the first time (movie edition, obviously).

But I also can't bear the thought of missing out.

It takes two elevators and several sets of stairs, but finally we step out onto the highest viewing platform in Paris. There's a protective grate, but I hang back. Up here, the air is colder, and I wonder if I'd be able to feel a sudden change in temperature—a warning, if that's what it was—before something goes wrong. The Eiffel Tower looks like it's held together with a million nuts and bolts. What would happen if one of them broke? Or a sudden gust of wind forced me toward the edge?

I shake my head to clear it. I'm starting to sound as paranoid as Jacob.

"You say paranoid, I say practical," counters Jacob.

And then, before I can protest, Mom links her arm through mine and draws me closer to the edge. As Dad rests his hand on my shoulder, I forget to be afraid. The entire city sprawls beneath me, as far as I can see, white, and gold, and green, and I know there is no photo in this world that can capture this view.

And for a moment, I forget about the ghosts that supposedly haunt this tower. For a moment, I *almost* forget the eerie, off-kilter feeling of being followed.

For a moment, Paris is simply magical.

"Just wait," says Jacob cheerfully. "I'm sure *something* will go wrong."

CHAPTER EIGHT

The crew hands Mom and Dad the day's footage so they can review it, and Pauline kisses each of us twice, once on each cheek, and slips away into the late-afternoon light. Mom and Dad decide we should have a picnic in the hotel room. We stop by a street market and buy bread, cheese, sausages, and fruit. Mom hums, shopping bags swinging from her fingers. Dad has a baguette under his arm, and I snap a photo of them, smiling to myself.

By the time we get back to the hotel, it feels like we've walked across the whole city. We climb to the room on aching legs, and I'm the last one through.

"Cass, get the door," says Mom, her arms full of food.

I nudge the door shut with my foot and tug the camera strap over my head, retreating to the little bedroom. Jacob and I flop down on my bed.

What a strange day, I think.

"Even stranger than usual," admits Jacob.

I roll over with a groan, and I'm just reaching for one of the comics in my bag when Mom's voice cuts through the suite.

"*Cassidy!*"

Jacob sits up. "That doesn't sound good."

My mom has a lot of voices. There's the *I'm proud of you* voice. The *You're late for dinner* voice. The *I need to talk to you about this life-changing decision your father and I have made* voice. And then there's the *You are in so much trouble* voice.

That's the one Mom's using.

I head into the main room and find her standing, arms crossed, by the hotel room door. It's open.

"What did I ask you to do?" she snaps, and I look from her to the door in confusion.

"I closed it!" I say, glancing toward Jacob, who only shrugs.

"Don't look at me," he says. "*I* didn't open it."

And I don't really understand the big deal until I hear Dad out in the hall, calling "Here, kitty, kitty" and rattling Grim's food dish.

Uh-oh.

"He got *out*?" I cry.

Here's the thing: Grim isn't a normal cat. He's not a hunter, and not even all that fast. Back home, he moved around about as much as a loaf of bread. So even if I *did* leave the door open, which I *know* I didn't, the chances of him going anywhere are slim to none.

And yet, he's not here.

And he's not in the hallway, either.

We split up. Dad makes his way up the stairs toward the third floor, Mom heads down to the lobby, and Jacob and I comb the space between.

How did he get out? *Why* did he get out? Grim's never shown much interest in the outside world—the few times he wandered beyond our front porch, he made it as far as the nearest patch of sun before sprawling out on his back to take a nap.

"Grim?" I call softly.

"Grim!" echoes Jacob.

My throat tightens a little. Where *is* he?

We look behind potted plants and under tables, but there's no sign of the cat on the second floor, or the first. No sign as we reach the lobby, where Mom's talking to the concierge, and I decide to check the salon where we had breakfast. It's out of service for the night, but one of the glass doors is open a crack. A gap just large enough for a cat.

I slip through, Jacob on my heels. I paw at the wall, searching for the light switch, but I can't find one. Even though the curtains have been pulled shut, the Rue de Rivoli shines through, just enough light to see by.

"Grim?" I call softly, trying to keep my voice steady as I creep between the tables.

And then, between one step and the next, I suck in a breath. It's like hitting a patch of cold air. A sudden shiver rolls through me.

"Jacob—"

Ding . . . ding . . . ding . . .

Jacob and I both look up. A chandelier hangs overhead, crystals chiming faintly as they sway.

Jacob and I glance at each other.

My look says, *Was that you?*

And his says, *Are you crazy?*

The cold gets worse, and as I watch, the tablecloth begins to slide from a nearby table, dragging the place settings with it. I lunge toward it, a fraction too late. The plates and silverware go crashing to the floor, and a second later, a shape darts through the darkness to my left. It's shadow on shadow, too dark to see, but one thing's for certain.

It's larger than a cat.

Before I can follow it, Jacob calls out, "Found him!"

I turn back, and see Jacob on his hands and knees on the other side of the room, looking beneath a chair.

Sure enough, there's Grim.

But when I get close, he hisses.

Grim *never* hisses, but now he looks up at me, his green eyes wide and his ears thrown back, fangs bared. And when I reach for him, he darts past me, through Jacob's outstretched hands and out of the salon. We chase after him into the lobby, where the very displeased desk clerk who checked us in yesterday catches him by the scruff of the neck.

She turns toward Mom.

"I believe," she says curtly, "this belongs to you."

Mom scowls at the cat. "I'm so sorry," she says, taking the thoroughly unhappy Grim, turning her glare on me. "It won't happen again."

But as I follow her back upstairs, all I can think is, *I'm sure I closed our door.*

Mom and Dad set out the makeshift picnic on the low coffee table, and the tension dissolves as we sit on pillows on the floor, eating apples and cheese and fresh baguette. As my parents discuss the day's filming, my mind wanders back again and again to the cold. I felt it at lunch, right before the awning broke, and again on the path in the gardens, and again downstairs in the salon. And every time, it came with the feeling, just as strong, that I wasn't alone.

Something certainly spooked Grim. He's handled it by collapsing into a fluffy mound, snoring softly at the foot of my bed.

What did he see? What did I see?

I think of the shadow in the salon. Maybe it was a trick of the eye, streetlights making shapes . . .

"You okay, Cass?" asks Mom. "You look a mile away."

I manage a smile. "Sorry," I say. "Just tired."

I push up from the table and grab my phone.

I need a second opinion.

I text Lara.

Me:
Can you talk?

Me:
Need help.

Ten seconds later, the phone rings.

I head for the bathroom, and Jacob follows me inside. He's careful to keep his back to the mirror as I close the door and answer.

"Cassidy Blake," says a prim English voice. "In trouble already?"

I hit the video chat button, and after a second of buffering, Lara Chowdhury appears on-screen. She's sitting in a high-back chair, a cup of tea balanced on a stack of books beside her.

Her attention flicks to Jacob. "I see you still have your pet ghost."

Jacob scowls. "Jealous you don't have one, too?"

"Lay off," I say, addressing both of them.

Lara sighs and leans her head on one hand. Her black hair is pulled up in a messy bun on top of her head. It's the first time anything about Lara could be described as *messy*, and—

"Are those . . . Harry Potter pajamas?" I ask.

She looks down at herself. "Just because they're blue and bronze—"

"They're *totally* Harry Potter pajamas, aren't they?"

Lara bristles. "They're *comfortable*. If they just *happen* to accurately represent my chosen house—" She shakes her head and changes course. "How's Paris?"

"Haunted."

"Tell me about it," she says. "I was there last summer, and I certainly had my hands full. Where have you been so far?"

"The Tuileries, the Luxembourg Gardens, the Eiffel Tower. Oh, and the Catacombs."

"You went into the *Catacombs*?" Lara sounds *almost* impressed.

"Yeah," I say. "It wasn't *that* bad. I mean, don't get me wrong, it wasn't a day at the beach, but with so many skeletons, I thought it would be worse . . ."

Lara shrugs. "Graveyards are usually pretty quiet."

"I know, but since the bodies were disturbed, I thought—"

"Oh, please," says Lara, "if ghosts got riled up every

time their bones were moved, there wouldn't be room in the in-between."

"But the Catacombs *are* haunted," I say.

"Of *course* they're haunted," says Lara. "All of Paris is haunted. But I'm sure the Catacombs aren't *six-million-angry-spirits* haunted." Lara straightens in her chair. "Well? You didn't call just to catch up."

"No." I chew my lip. "Something weird is going on."

I tell her about the awning breaking at lunch, the sense of being followed, Grim getting out, and the tablecloth that moved in the salon—not to mention the shadow. And I tell her about the cold rush I felt right before each one.

Lara's eyes narrow as I talk. "Cassidy," she says slowly, when I'm done. "You might have attracted a *poltergeist*."

She sounds nervous. Which makes me nervous.

"What's a poltergeist?" asks Jacob.

"It's a spirit drawn to spectral energy," says Lara, keeping her attention on me. "It was probably dormant until it sensed yours, Cassidy." Her eyes flick toward Jacob. "Or *his*. That cold sensation you've been feeling, it *is* a kind of intuition, a warning that strong spirits are near."

"Okay," I say, perching on the bathtub. "But a poltergeist is just a kind of ghost, right?"

"A very *dangerous* kind of ghost," says Lara. "They feed on chaos."

"Cassidy!" calls Mom, knocking on the door. "Everything all right in there?"

"Yep!" I call back. "Just brushing my teeth." I lower my voice as I turn back to Lara. "But how can a poltergeist cause trouble in the real world? Shouldn't it be locked in the Veil?"

Lara pinches the bridge of her nose. "Poltergeists are *wanderers*. They're not stuck in a loop or a memory, and they aren't tied to the place they died. They've come loose from the in-between. They can move freely through it, and even reach across the Veil into our world."

"Like the Raven in Red," I say, recalling the ghostly woman who haunted Edinburgh, stealing its children before she stole my life.

"Yes," says Lara. "And no. Even the Raven couldn't leave the in-between until she had your life. That's why she had to lure you in. But poltergeists already have one foot on either side. So congratulations, you've managed to wake something even more dangerous."

My stomach drops at the thought. The Raven wasn't exactly a piece of cake.

"It's like a video game," says Jacob, "where the boss on each level is harder to beat."

Lara frowns. "That's an overly simplistic way of looking at this. But I suppose so."

"Okay," I say, mind spinning. "But a poltergeist is still a spirit. So I just need to find it and send it back."

"Yes," says Lara. "As soon as possible. Poltergeists start with little things, acts of mischief, but eventually they turn to menace and then mayhem. Violence." I think of the torn awning, the glass shattering on the table, how lucky I was I didn't get cut. "They don't have any qualms about hurting people, even *killing* them," warns Lara. "And the more trouble a poltergeist causes, the more powerful they get." She looks to Jacob, and then back at me, her next words pointed. "Spirits this strong have no place in our world, Cassidy. Every minute they're loose, they cause damage to the balance, and the Veil."

Jacob looks down at the floor, hands closing into fists. We both know she's talking about more than the poltergeist.

I clear my throat. "Well, great," I say, "thanks for the pep talk. Sure you don't want to make a trip down to Paris?"

A sad smile flickers across Lara's face. "I wish," she says. "But I'm here, if you need me. And, Cassidy?"

"Yeah?"

"Do be careful. And, *you*"—she glares at Jacob—"as long as you're here, make yourself useful."

She hangs up, and I'm left staring down at the darkened screen.

"You know," says Jacob dryly, "I think she's starting to like me."

I sigh and kick him out so I can brush my teeth for real.

I need my sleep—tomorrow I'm going to hunt a poltergeist.

By the time I climb into bed, Jacob's nowhere to be seen. He doesn't stick around at night, but the truth is, I don't know where he goes.

Sometimes, even psychic ghost best friends have secrets.

CHAPTER NINE

Something jerks me out of a heavy, dreamless sleep.

I don't know what it is—a weight on the edge of my bed, Grim walking around—only that I'm awake, and the room is dark. The night is still thick beyond my window. My door is ajar, and I hold my breath and listen, straining to hear something, anything—Dad's snoring, the ambient sounds of late-night tourists on the street—but the suite is unnaturally quiet.

Until I hear the click of a lock, the faint groan of the hotel door swinging open.

The poltergeist.

Thin red light spills in from the hall, and I'm on my feet, padding barefoot through the dark. By the time I reach the doorway, the crimson glow is sliding down the stairs. I step into the hall and reach for my mirror pendant, only to realize I'm not wearing it. I must have left the necklace on the bedside table. As I turn back to get it, the hotel door swings shut, locking me out.

A draft rolls down the hall, sudden and cold, and I fight back a shiver.

"Cassidy . . ."

My name is a whisper on the air, faint and far away, but I know that voice.

"Jacob?" I call out, trying to keep my voice low.

"Cassidy . . ." he calls again, his voice drifting up through the floor. Something crashes, and I hurry toward the stairs, sure that the poltergeist has Jacob, that he's in danger.

Hold on, Jacob, I think, plunging down the stairs. *Hold on, hold on.*

They don't have any qualms about hurting people, Lara said.

Hold on.

With every downward step, the temperature falls.

By the second floor, I'm cold.

By the first, I'm shivering.

"Jacob?" I call again, my breath fogging in front of me as I reach the lobby, slipping on the marble floor. I scramble to my feet, ready to fight, ready to save my best friend—

But there's no one else here.

No poltergeist attacking him, only Jacob, on his knees in the center of the lobby. His head is in his hands as the air around him churns into a frenzy. The chandelier swings, and the paintings shake, and a chair scrapes across the floor, and I realize with horror that all of it is coming from *him*.

"Jacob!" I shout over the howling wind. "Can you hear me?"

He lets out a low groan. "What's happening to me?" His voice sounds strange and hollow. "Cassidy . . ."

He trails off, the color seeping out of his clothes, his skin. Water drips from his hair, his jeans, pooling around him on the marble floor until he looks the way he did that one time I saw him in a mirror.

He looks gray and wet and lost.

He looks *dead*.

No. No. No.

"Cassidy!" calls a voice, but it's not coming from Jacob. It's *Lara*.

She's standing behind the front desk, bracing herself against the worst of the chaos, her black braid whipping in the wind. Lara, who always seems to have an answer, who always knows what to do. But her eyes aren't wide with worry. They're furious.

"I warned you this would happen!" she calls, her voice warping from the force of Jacob's whirlwind. "I told you he was getting stronger."

I duck as a vase shatters against the pillar over my head, raining down shards of glass and broken flowers that are then yanked back up before they ever hit the marble floor.

"Cass!" screams Lara as the chaos in the lobby reaches a high, keening pitch. "You have to send him on."

But I can't. I won't. There has to be another way.

Jacob curls in on himself at the center of the storm, and I try to get closer, to grab his hand, to pull him back from wherever he is. I can save him. I know if I can just get close enough—but the whirlwind around him is too strong, and it slams me backward until I hit a marble pillar and—

I sit up, gasping in the dark.

It was just a bad dream.

"You're acting weird," says Jacob the next morning.

He looks like Jacob again. No ghoulish face, no empty

eyes, no pool of water at his feet, just my best friend in all his semitransparent glory. I wish I could throw my arms around him. Instead, I do my best to clear my mind, grateful he can't read my dreams as well as my thoughts.

"Just tired," I say as we step off the Metro.

The truth is, my morning isn't off to the best start.

I nearly jumped out of my chair at breakfast when someone in the salon dropped a coffeepot. No spirit activity there, just a server with slippery fingers. I know not *everything* is a portent of danger, but it still put me on edge.

I tried to shake it off, but it only got worse. As we were leaving the hotel, a car alarm went off down the street. And then another, and another, the horns blaring like dominoes.

"Bit nervous this morning?" asked Dad, patting my shoulder as I squinted through the crowded sidewalk, trying to catch sight of whoever triggered the first one. I thought about cutting through the Veil—but I couldn't, not in front of my parents, Pauline, and the film crew.

Now we step through the cemetery gates, and I feel the temperature dip.

"Are you catching a cold?" asks Mom when she sees me pull my sweater close against the chill.

"Maybe," I say, shoving my hands in my pockets and clutching the mirror necklace. I feel like my nerves are wound tight enough to—

A tree branch crashes to the ground on the path in front of us.

Mom jumps, her arm holding me back.

"That was close," she says, looking down at the branch.

"Way too close," I mutter.

What was it Lara said? First comes mischief, then menace, then mayhem.

I need to take care of things before they escalate.

And a graveyard seems like a good place to start.

I study the large paper unfolded in Mom's hands.

"What kind of cemetery needs a map?" I ask.

She beams at me, eyes bright. "A very, very big one."

That, it turns out, is an understatement.

Père Lachaise is like a city within a city. There are even street signs, blocks, neighborhoods. Cobbled paths wind between graves. Some graves are low, like stone caskets, and others looming, like small houses side by side. Some of the crypts are new and others are old, some sealed while others yawn open, and here and there old trees threaten to unbury tombs, roots pushing up between—and beneath—the stone.

There's no anger in this place.

Just a shallow wave of sadness, and loss.

"Cass," says Mom, "don't wander off."

And for once, it doesn't feel like an idle warning. This place is *huge*, and it's too easy to imagine getting lost. But that also means my parents won't notice if I slip away.

I fall back a little with every step, finally stopping to linger among the tombstones.

If I were a poltergeist, where would I be?

"Here, ghosty ghosty," calls Jacob.

I look up and see him perching on a large stone angel, one leg dangling over the edge and the other drawn up, his elbow resting on his knee. As I lift the camera to snap a photo, he strikes a pensive posture, surveying the cemetery.

The camera clicks, and I wonder if he'll show up on the film.

There was a time when I knew he wouldn't. Now I'm not so sure. I think of the last photo from Edinburgh, the one I keep tucked in the pocket of my camera bag. In it,

Jacob and I are standing on opposite sides of a window. Me in the shop and him on the street, each of us turning to look at the other.

He's not *really* there, in the glass.

But he's not *not* there, either.

It could have been a trick of the light, a warped reflection.

But I don't think it was.

Spirits this strong have no place in our world.

Lara's warning fuses with her words from my nightmare.

You have to send him on.

Jacob clears his throat.

"Well," he says, jumping down from his perch. "No poltergeist."

"No," I say, looking around. "Not here . . ."

Jacob frowns. "I don't like the way you said that."

Up ahead, Mom and Dad stop in front of a crypt, Anton and Annette readying their cameras, and I see my chance. I tug the mirror from my pocket.

"Come on," I whisper, reaching for the Veil. "If the poltergeist won't come to us, we'll go to the poltergeist."

CHAPTER TEN

I'm plunged from something into nothing and back again, all in the time it takes to blink.

My feet land back on the cobblestone path, and Père Lachaise stretches out again, a ghost of its former self. Tendrils of fog curl around my legs, and the cemetery is vast and gray and eerily still. I draw the mirror from my pocket, wrapping the cord around my wrist as Jacob appears beside me. He looks around, nose crinkling a little.

"What is it with graveyards and mist?" he asks, kicking at the cloudy air around our feet.

"A-plus for atmosphere," I say.

Nearby, a crypt door swings on a broken hinge. Across the path, a crow caws and takes flight.

"I'll take creepy Halloween soundtracks for two hundred," mutters Jacob.

But for all the moodiness of this place, it's quiet.

The thing about cemeteries is that they're not as haunted as you'd think. Sure, there are a few ghosts here and there, but most restless spirits are bound to the place where they *died*, not the place where they're buried.

So it shouldn't be that hard to find our restless spirit.

As long as it wants to be found.

"And if it doesn't?" asks Jacob.

Which is a good question.

How *do* you lure out a poltergeist?

"Maybe if we ignore it, it'll just lose interest in us and go away."

"It's not a *bee*, Jacob. And you heard Lara. The longer the poltergeist is out, the more chaos it will cause. Which is bad on its own, and worse since this particular spirit seems intent on bothering *us*."

I scan the tombs.

"Hello?" I call out, gripping the mirror pendant.

"What do you think a poltergeist looks like?" whispers Jacob. "Is it human? A monster? An octopus?"

"An octopus?"

He shrugs. "More arms, more misch—"

I lurch toward him, pressing my hand over his mouth. His eyebrows shoot up in confusion.

I heard something.

We stand, perfectly silent, perfectly still. And then it comes again.

A child's voice.

"*Un . . . deux . . . trois . . .*" it says in a singsong way.

The graveyard begins to fill with a soft red light, and a cold wind blows over my skin.

I can hear the shuffle of steps, small shoes skittering across a path. I turn just in time to see a shadow dart between the crypts.

". . . *quatre . . . cinq . . .*" the voice continues, and I really wish I spoke French.

"Come out!" I call. "I just want to talk."

". . . *sept . . .*" continues the voice, now behind me.

I spin, but there's no one there, only tombstones.

". . . *huit . . .*" Its voice is softer now, drifting away, taking the strange red light with it.

"Pretty shy for a spirit," says Jacob.

I chew my lip. He's right. For all the tricks the poltergeist has pulled, I haven't caught more than a glimpse of it. And if I want to catch this ghost, I'm going to have to get it to come to me.

"How do you plan on doing *that*?" asks Jacob. "Do you have any poltergeist bait lying around?"

I rub my temples. What did Lara say?

They thrive on creating trouble. Making mischief.

Okay. So I just need to give the ghost a chance to make some. I look up at the crypts, some of them as tall as houses.

Jacob reads my mind, and then says, *"No."*

"This is a terrible idea," says Jacob as I hoist myself up on top of the grave.

"You always say that."

I look down. I'm only two or three feet off the ground. Not high enough. I grab the carved corner of the nearest crypt and begin to climb higher.

"Yeah, and I'm usually right," he calls up. "What does that say about your ideas?"

My shoes slip on the side of the crypt, but finally I haul myself up and straighten, balancing on the gabled roof. I scan the graveyard.

"Come out, come out, wherever you are," I call.

Nothing happens.

I will myself to walk along the pointing roof, moving closer to the edge. I hold my breath and wait.

"Oh well," says Jacob, shifting from foot to foot, "you tried your best. Guess you better come on down and . . ." He trails off as the voice returns, suddenly *much* closer.

"*. . . dix.*"

A flush of cold brushes my skin and a tile slips somewhere behind me, shattering on a tombstone below. The sound sends spectral crows into flight, and I turn toward the crash and see him, standing on the top of a tombstone ten feet away.

The poltergeist.

I don't know what I expected.

A monster, perhaps. A shadow creature seven feet tall, all claws and teeth.

But it's just a boy.

A little kid, maybe six or seven, with curly brown hair and a round face smudged with dirt. He's dressed in old-fashioned clothes, a button-down shirt and trousers that bunch around his bony knees. His edges flicker a little, as if he's not entirely here, but it's his eyes that stop me.

They aren't brown, or blue, but *red*.

The red of a burning ember, or a flashlight against a palm. The kind of red that *glows*, casting a crimson light on the graves, and the crypts, and the fog.

"Found you," I say, and the boy smiles at me, right before he *moves*. Not the way a boy should be able to move, one foot in front of the other. No. It's like he's not bound by the rules of this place, and in the time it takes me to blink, he skips forward. One second he's standing on a crypt ten feet away. The next, he's a foot away, perching on the gabled roof.

"Now!" urges Jacob, and my hand flies up, the mirror pendant right in front of the boy's face.

His red eyes widen as he gazes into the glass, lost in his reflection.

"Watch and listen," I recite. "See and know. This is what you are."

I reach for the thread in his chest, but when my hand hits his shirt, it doesn't go through. He's still solid, or as close as a ghost can get. I clear my throat, my fingers tightening on the mirror as I start again.

"Watch and listen," I say, trying to make my voice forceful. "See and—"

But the boy frowns, his red eyes flicking from the mirror up to my face, as if it has no hold on him.

That's not possible, I think.

Right before he shoves me off the roof.

PART THREE

MENACE

CHAPTER ELEVEN

There's this moment when you start to fall, when you think, *Maybe everything will be okay.*

Maybe I'll catch my balance. Maybe a hand will steady me. Maybe something soft will break my fall.

In this case, it doesn't.

I'm falling, and somewhere between the edge of the roof and the lawn below, I cross back through the Veil and land *hard* on the ground beside the crypt. The fall knocks all the air from my lungs and sends pain jolting up through my right arm, and for a second all I can do is blink away the stars and hope I didn't break anything.

Jacob appears, looming over me, and he's worried enough that the first words out of his mouth aren't even "I told you so" but "Are you okay?"

I sit up, dazed, and grateful that my head missed the sharp corner of the nearest tombstone. My elbow zings and my fingers tingle, but as far as I can tell, I haven't broken anything. Including my camera.

Small miracles.

I groan, wishing Jacob were solid enough to help me to my feet. Instead, I get up, rubbing my arm. "I'm okay."

"Good," says Jacob, glancing back toward the crypt. "What happened up there?"

I look up, and for a second I can still see the boy's outline, a faint impression of the poltergeist scowling down at me from the roof. An afterimage, like a flash, against my eyes, but when I blink, it's gone.

"The mirror didn't work."

"Why not?" presses Jacob. "Is it busted? Or fogged up or something?"

I check, but my reflection looks back, sharp and clear—and confused.

"What about the words?" asks Jacob. "Did you say them right?"

I did. I did *everything* right.

So why didn't it work?

I loop the necklace over my head and tuck the pendant

beneath my collar. And then I do the only thing I can think of.

I call Lara.

"Wait, wait, slow down," she says.

Jacob and I have been talking over each other from the moment Lara picked up the phone. "What do you *mean* the mirror didn't work?"

I walk faster, scouring the graveyard in case my parents are close by. "I mean, it didn't *work*."

Voices rise up somewhere to my right. Mom and Dad.

"Well, you must have done something wrong," says Lara. I spot my parents down one of the branching paths, narrating in front of a tombstone while Anton and Annette film them.

"I did everything you taught me," I snap. Pauline looks over her shoulder and holds a slim, manicured finger to her lips. "I cornered the poltergeist," I say, lowering my voice. "I held up the mirror, I said the words, and then he just *looked up*. At my face."

"And then he pushed her off a roof!" adds Jacob.

"What were you doing on a roof?" demands Lara.

"It doesn't matter," I hiss, rubbing my arm, which is still sore from the fall. "What matters is that this poltergeist is still out there, and he's apparently *immune to mirrors*."

Lara exhales, and I can practically *hear* her pinching the bridge of her nose.

"Okay, okay," she says softly, obviously talking more to herself than to me. "I'll go talk to Uncle Weathershire and call you back. In the meantime, just stay *out* of the Veil, and on your guard."

As if on cue, the corner of a tombstone crumbles near the film crew. Anton jumps out of the way and nearly falls through the glass of an open crypt door.

Jacob and I exchange a look, and then turn toward the phone, and Lara.

"Hurry."

"Come on, Lara," I mutter, tapping the phone against my palm.

It's been an hour, and she still hasn't called back.

The crew finished filming at Père Lachaise, and we headed for the Metro. Now I hold my breath as we make our way down to the platform, waiting for something to go wrong, hoping it won't. It's stuffy on the train, but I lie to Mom, telling her I'm cold, and she lends me the extra sweater she always keeps in her bag. I wrap it around me, pulling it close even though I'm sweating under all the fabric.

"What exactly are you doing?" asks Jacob as my cheeks flush from the heat.

So far the only warning I have that the poltergeist is near is that flush of cold. I want to be sure I can feel it.

"You're turning yourself into a ghost thermometer."

I pull the sleeves down over my hands. *Basically.*

The lights flicker overhead, and I nearly jump out of my seat. But there's no flash of cold, no warning chill, and a second later the lights come back on.

"That happens sometimes on trains," says Mom, scooting closer. "But don't worry. I doubt this car is haunted."

She says it breezily, but my stomach tightens, a reminder that the poltergeist isn't the only thing I have to worry about. The Veil is still ebbing and flowing around me, ready to drag me under the second I let my guard down. Jacob inches closer until our shoulders almost touch.

"Not on my watch," he says.

We get off at a station called Opéra and step onto the street in front of a giant stone building with more piping than a wedding cake. This, according to Dad, is the Palais Garnier. The Paris Opera House.

"I thought *The Phantom of the Opera* was just a Broadway show," I say.

"It is," says Dad.

"But you're saying there really *is* a phantom here?"

"I'm saying there's a story."

"Most tales are inspired by *something*," says Mom, craning her neck.

We walk inside the opera house. The entire gallery is made of marble, the swirls of white-and-gray stone interrupted only by massive iron candelabras. The stairs are straight out of Hogwarts, giant steps that split off to the left and the right, as if leading up to the house common rooms. As we step into the auditorium, Jacob lets out a low, appreciative whistle. It's full of red velvet seats and balconies, every surface covered in gold.

Mom, Dad, Pauline, and the crew head down into the chambers *beneath* the opera. I decide to sit this one out, sinking into one of the velvet seats with the leftover macarons from yesterday. Dad shoots me one last *stay put* look as they retreat down the aisle.

I watch as a handful of workers onstage maneuver pieces of a set. I get glimpses of the unfinished bits, the cables and ropes and undersides exposed. Soon, the set pieces come together into what looks like the front of a mansion.

"This is nice," says Jacob, perching beside me. "We should do this more often, the whole *not*-looking-for-ghosts thing."

"We're not *not* looking for ghosts," I say, thoughts turning.

Every crack of the stagehand's hammer, every scrape of wood, every creak and groan puts me on edge.

When my cell rings, I yelp in surprise and bang my knee against the arm of the seat.

I answer, rubbing my shin. "Hey."

"Is for horses," chides Lara.

"What?"

"Never mind, just something my mother says. Can you talk? Where are you?"

"The opera."

"Oh, have you seen the phantom? There are actually *several*. Uncle told me to leave them alone, though—they weren't causing any trouble, and apparently a few ghosts can be good for business. Don't know if I agree with him, but I figured the phantoms could wait till my next school trip."

Jacob clears his throat.

"Anyway," says Lara pointedly, "do you want the bad news, or the bad news?"

"I don't think that's how the saying goes," comments Jacob.

"Well, it's how it goes now. Because we—or rather *you*—have a very large problem."

"Great," I say, because I don't seem to have enough of those. "Care to explain?"

Lara clears her throat. "Remember how I said poltergeists are stronger than normal ghosts because they aren't bound to the Veil?"

"Yes."

"And as you already know, the Veil is tailored to fit the ghost, the place they died, which means it's essentially tied to the ghost's *memory*—that's what binds it there. So if a poltergeist *isn't* bound to the Veil, it's because—"

"They don't remember," I say as it hits me.

Lara exhales. "Exactly. That's why the mirror didn't do anything to stop him. A reflection only works on ghosts because it shows them what they already know but simply haven't accepted."

Watch and listen. See and know. This is what you are.

"But if someone showed you something you *didn't* remember," continues Lara, "it wouldn't have the same impact on you."

"But if the mirror doesn't work," says Jacob, "how are we supposed to *stop* him?"

"It doesn't work," says Lara, "because he doesn't remember who he was. Which means you have to remind him."

"And how are we supposed to do that?" I ask. "It's not like we have any clue who he is—was."

"Well," says Lara, "what do you already know about him?"

"Nothing," I hiss, exasperated.

"Don't be ridiculous. You've *seen* him, haven't you? What does he look like?"

I close my eyes, trying to summon the only clear image I have, from the moment I was balanced on top of the grave. "He was short, only came up to my shoulder."

"Okay, so he's young."

"He had brown hair. Old-fashioned clothes."

"What *kind* of old-fashioned?"

"I don't *know*," I say. "The kind with buttons."

Lara makes a short, exasperated sound. "Well, next time, pay more attention. Every detail is a clue. What he looks like, when he started following you, what he said—"

"Wait," says Jacob. "He did say something. Remember, Cass . . . ?" Jacob trails off, trying to sound out the words. "Un, du, twa, something about a 'cat sank' . . ." he fumbles, then adds, "The last word was definitely *dees*."

"Well done, ghost," says Lara grudgingly. "All right, that's interesting."

"Do you know what it means?" I ask.

"He was *counting*," says Lara. "*Un, deux, trois, quatre, cinq, six, sept, huit, neuf, dix*. That's one through ten in French." She lowers her voice, talking to herself as much as us. "But why would he be counting *up* instead of *down*?"

"You speak French?" I cut in.

"Of course," says Lara briskly. "And German. They make us take two foreign languages in school. I also know a little Punjabi, thanks to my dad. My parents say language is the most valuable currency. Don't *you* know any other language?"

"I know how to ask for the bathroom in Spanish," offers Jacob.

"Um." I chew my lip. "I memorized all the incantations in Harry Potter." I look at Jacob. "And I can speak to ghosts."

"Obviously not," says Lara, "or you wouldn't need me to translate. Look, until we find out who this poltergeist is—*was*—you don't stand a chance of winning."

"Thanks for the confidence," I mutter as the film crew reappears, Mom and Dad in the lead. Anton and Annette follow, cameras hoisted on their shoulders as my parents make their way down the aisle toward the stage. They're shooting B-roll, the snippets of footage that will go behind a voiceover, help set the scene.

"I suggest," Lara is saying, "you start by figuring out where he came from, how he died. Call me when you have a solid lead. And, Cassidy?"

"Yeah, I know. Be careful."

We both hang up, and I stand, picking my way through the seats. I play Lara's conversation again in my head.

"Hey, Jacob," I say. "You remember, don't you?"

His face darkens a little. "Remember what?"

I swallow. "Who you were, before. How you . . ." I don't say the word, but I think it. *Died*. Jacob's face shutters like a window, all the color and humor suddenly gone.

"Are you serious?"

"I'm just asking."

"I'm not a *poltergeist*, Cassidy," he snaps, the hair rising around his face.

I shiver, suddenly cold, and for a second, I think the chill is coming from *him* before something snaps onstage and a massive piece of the set begins to fall forward.

Straight toward my parents.

CHAPTER TWELVE

L ook out!" I scream, already running.

"Cass, wait!" calls Jacob as I leap over a seat and into the aisle.

Mom and Dad turn toward me and then look up, their eyes wide as the wooden frame tips forward. Shouts go up across the stage, and I crash into my parents, hoping to force them out of the way, but at the last second, the massive set piece shudders to a halt. It stops a few feet above our heads, half a dozen ropes and cables pulled tight.

"*Désolé!*" calls a stagehand. Pauline shakes her head and answers in a flurry of French, sounding furious.

The tirade goes on for several long seconds before she shakes her head and turns back toward us. "Theater."

Mom laughs, a breathy, relieved sound, and Dad pats my shoulder. I must be looking as shaken up as I feel because he soothes me, saying, "It's okay, Cass. We're all okay."

"That's why they have more than one rope," adds Mom.

But my heart is still pounding in my chest as I follow my parents outside onto the street. They could have been hurt. They could have been *killed*.

I swallow. One thing is for sure: The poltergeist is after *me*, not my parents. If we split up, then at least *they'll* be out of harm's way.

"And we'll be right in it," says Jacob. "Besides," he adds, waving a hand at my parents, "how exactly are we supposed to get away from the Inspecters here?"

Good question.

My mind races as I try to think. Then we round a corner, and I slow down at the sight of a movie theater.

I have an idea.

Most of the movies are in French, of course. The only ones showing in English are a horror film—no thank you—and a teen rom-com, one of those generic feel-good stories, the poster featuring a girl with a series of boys in thought bubbles over her head.

And there's a showing in ten minutes.

I stop, admiring the poster. "I've been wanting to see this," I say softly, as if to myself.

Mom wraps an arm around my shoulder. "Since when do you like rom-coms?"

I shrug. "I don't know. Lara told me about it." She didn't, of course, but as far as lies go, it's pretty innocent. "It seems fun. Maybe I'm just feeling a little ghosted-out. This is my summer vacation, after all. And Paris is amazing, but I just— I'd really love to do something *normal*." I point to the start time. "There's even a showing now." I look up at her. "Can I go? You can pick me up later."

Mom sulks. "But we're going to the Rue des Chantres! You wouldn't want to miss that."

I bite my lip and let my shoulders fall. "I guess not."

Jacob claps his hands at my Oscar-worthy performance. Mom and Dad exchange a glance, and then a few quiet words, before Mom nods and says, "Okay."

I throw my arms around her shoulders. "Thank you."

Dad slides a few bills through the ticket window, and he even gives me some cash for a soda and popcorn.

"We'll be back," he says, "*before* the movie ends." He points to the sidewalk. "Right here."

I wave goodbye and head inside, buying a snack at the counter, letting the usher tear my ticket. He points to the first theater on the left, and Jacob and I make our way into the darkened theater.

"A movie," Jacob says, sinking into the leather seat. "This is a nice change of pace."

I sip my soda and check my phone, waiting for one minute to pass, then two. I set a timer on my phone for two hours.

Jacob watches me. "We're not staying for the movie, are we?"

I get up, leaving the bucket of popcorn at my feet. "Nope."

Jacob sighs. "Just once," he says, "I wish we'd do the normal thing."

I push open the door marked EXIT, and we slip down the hall and out onto the Paris street.

"Where's the fun in that?"

Paris is a *big* city, and as we stand on the street, blocks stretching in every direction, two hours suddenly doesn't seem like very much time.

"Time to do what?" asks Jacob, for once unable to make sense of my jumbled thoughts.

I don't blame him. My head is spinning with everything I know and everything I *don't*.

I have to remind the poltergeist who he is—was.

In order to do that, I have to figure out who he is—was.

In order to do that, I have to find out more about him.

In order to do that . . .

I take a deep breath and reach for the Veil, pulling the curtain aside before Jacob can even think to protest.

I step out of the world, into a moment of free fall, like a missed step, a lurch of darkness. Then Paris settles around me again, stranger, grayer, *older*. The buildings look different, no longer uniform rows of pale stone but mismatched, like a ragged hem.

I cup my hands around my mouth and call, at the top of my lungs, "HEY, GHOST!"

The words echo away into the fog. I take a breath and shout.

"COME OUT, COME OUT, WHEREVER YOU AR—"

Jacob appears, clapping a hand over my mouth.

"What are you doing?" he hisses.

I pull free. "I'm tired of letting *him* call all the shots. I don't want to do this on his terms anymore. I want to do it on mine."

"So your best idea is to shout until he shows up?"

"We need a better look at him, right?"

"Yeah," says Jacob, "but last time you came face-to-face, he pushed you off a roof."

"Well, this time, my feet are on the ground. Besides . . ." I trail off. Over Jacob's shoulder, a shadow is taking shape in the fog, moving toward us.

But when the figure parts the mist, it isn't the poltergeist.

It's a man in an old-fashioned suit. He lifts an old-fashioned pistol and aims it straight at me, and Jacob wrenches me back out of the Veil before the shot goes off.

I crash through a wave of cold water before landing on my butt on the curb in present-day Paris. Jacob looms over me, folding his arms. "You really should have seen that coming."

I get to my feet, brushing off my jeans, and start walking.

As soon as I think I'm far enough away from the ghost with the gun, I take a deep breath and reach for the Veil again.

"Wait—" starts Jacob, but he's too late.

I'm already through.

A shudder, a plunge, a second of darkness, and I'm back in the in-between.

The Veil is different here, the city still old-fashioned but a little newer than last time.

There's a bridge just ahead, a stone arch garnished with statues and lampposts. As I start across it, a carriage rattles past the other way, pulled by a pair of glossy black horses.

A man plays an accordion along the banks of the Seine below, the music high and thin, as if carried on a breeze.

A pair of women walk arm in arm in fancy dresses, the skirts as wide as the sidewalk, their heads bowed as they whisper.

I pull the mirror pendant from my back pocket and wrap it around my palm as I walk, willing the ghosts not to notice. Their eyes flick toward me, as if they know I don't belong, but they don't come after me, and I don't go after them.

"You know the definition of insanity, right?" asks Jacob, appearing beside me. "It's doing the same thing over and over again, and expecting a different result."

"I'm not doing the same thing," I point out. "You're right, shouting was a bad idea."

"Great," says Jacob. "So what's your new strategy?"

"I'm taking a walk."

"To where?"

"The end of the Veil."

I reach the other side of the bridge, and a block or so later, the in-between finally shifts again, thinning between one ghost's Veil and the next, until it's nothing but an empty stretch, a seam, a place where no ordinary ghost can go. But a poltergeist, a spirit not bound to the Veil . . .

I stand there, the blue-white light shining from my chest like a beacon.

Come out, come out, I think.

But there's no sign of him, or anyone else.

"Maybe he's playing hard to get," observes Jacob.

The words ping inside my head, landing on something, a thought I can't quite reach. I'm starting to get light-headed from the time in the Veil, the air thinning in my lungs.

I groan in exasperation and cut back into the land of the living, sagging onto a bench to steady myself.

Think. Think. Think.

Jacob sinks down beside me.

"It wasn't a bad idea," he says, trying to comfort me and also clearly hoping I'll give up, and we can go watch the rest of the movie.

But I can't. I'm *almost* onto something. The poltergeist has been staying close to me this whole time, so there's no reason to believe he's totally disappeared now. No, he must be hanging back, waiting. For what?

Playing hard to get.

Playing.

I straighten and look at Jacob. "I think you're right!"

He crosses his arms. "Don't sound so surprised." And then he adds, "Right about what?"

But I'm already on my feet, reaching for the Veil.

The world vanishes, springs back, and I steady myself against a lamppost, already dizzy—it's like diving for pennies on the bottom of a pool. Hold your breath, go down one too many times, and it gets harder to come back up. But this time, instead of shouting or searching, I look around the bleak gray world and find the front of a building, decorated by pillars.

I tug Jacob behind the nearest one and crouch low, pressing my camera to my chest to smother the light.

A few seconds later I feel cold air on the back of my neck, and I nearly jump before I realize it's just Jacob.

"You're breathing on me," I whisper, trying not to shiver.

"Sorry," he whispers back. "But what exactly are we doing?"

"We're hiding," I say.

All this time, the poltergeist has been playing a game. And so far, he's made all the rules. All this time, he's been following *us*. So why don't we follow *him*? Maybe he'll lead us somewhere. Maybe we'll find a clue. Maybe we'll figure out—

"That's a whole lot of maybes," says Jacob.

"Maybe is a match in the dark," I murmur, half to myself.

It's one of Mom's favorite sayings, for when she gets stuck on a story. She starts giving herself options, potential threads, turning every dead end into a new path with one simple word: *maybe*.

Maybe is a rope in a hole, or the key to a door.

Maybe is how you find the way out.

We just have to wait for him to show up.

We wait. One minute. Three. Five.

Until my head begins to pound, until it's hard for me to breathe. A reminder that I shouldn't be here; I'm not made of the right stuff.

But I *swear* I can feel the poltergeist nearby, a trickle of cold creeping through the air.

"Cassidy," warns Jacob, but I don't move.

Just a little longer.

"*Cass.*"

I'm sure he'll show up.

My vision blurs a little, and when I try to swallow, I taste the river in my throat. Panic ripples through me as I try to breathe, try to stand, but the Veil sways and darkness sweeps across my eyes, followed by nothing.

CHAPTER THIRTEEN

The next thing I know I'm sitting on the curb back in the real world, cars zooming through a busy intersection, the city full of color and noise. My head thuds dully, and I press my palms into my eyes and then look up, a translucent Jacob looming over me.

"Enough," he says, arms crossed. "That was way too close."

"It could have worked," I mumble, getting to my feet. "It would have if—"

I'm cut off by a sudden, violent shiver, and an instant later, a truck swerves around the corner.

I catch the briefest glimpse of a shadow before the truck's back door falls open and the contents begin to spill out. Boxes and crates smash into the street, followed by a massive golden frame that hurtles straight toward me.

The crack of wood.

The glint of glass.

Move, I think, but my legs are frozen.

"...*CAS*..."

Jacob calls my name, but the word is all stretched out and slow.

"...*SI*..."

Everything's too slow.

"...*DY*...!"

Everything except for the breaking pane of glass crashing toward me.

"Look out!"

And then something hits me. Not the frame, but a pair of hands. They plant themselves against my back and shove, and I stumble forward to the pavement, scraping my palms as the frame crashes into the stone wall and rains glass onto the street behind me.

I twist around and see Jacob standing there, amid the shattered glass. And before I can wonder how he was able to do that, I look down at his feet and realize it's not ordinary glass at all.

It's a *mirror*.

A thousand fragments littering the pavement at his feet.

"Don't look!" I call, but it's too late.

Jacob looks down.

His blue eyes widen. His whole body ripples, thins, the way it did the last time he saw himself, trapped in a reflection. A ghostly pallor begins to bleed across his front, hair darkening with water.

But then—somehow—Jacob tears free.

He shudders, and squeezes his eyes shut, and disappears, a faint flutter of gray in the air around him the only hint as to where he's gone.

The Veil.

People on the street are rushing forward, but before they reach me, I'm on my feet, grabbing for the thin gray curtain. I throw it aside, rushing through after Jacob. A brief second of falling, and then I'm on my feet. The Veil stretches, quiet and gray. It's thin here, the details faded, an in-between in the in-between. A place that doesn't belong to any one ghost.

There are places where the Veil is nothing, a stretch of blank paper. But Paris is too haunted for that, and even here, the Veil isn't quite empty. A faint impression of the city, ghosted on the pale surface. And of course, there's one thing in perfect detail.

Jacob.

He stands still, breathing heavily as he presses his palms against his eyes.

"Jacob?" I ask, trying to keep my voice light.

He doesn't answer, but the pallor is gone from his skin, the traces of damp erased from his clothes and hair.

"Jacob," I say again, and this time he lets out a shaky breath and straightens, hands falling away from his eyes.

"I'm fine," he says.

"How did you do that?" I ask, and I honestly don't know if I'm talking about the fact he *pushed* me or the fact he pulled himself free from his own reflection.

He just shakes his head.

"Jacob—"

"I said I'm *fine*." The tremor is gone from his voice, replaced by something I almost never hear. Annoyance. Anger. His hair flutters slightly, as if caught in a breeze. I open my mouth, but before I can say anything else, I feel it.

Cold.

A chill, pressed between my shoulder blades. I turn, and so does Jacob. And there, half a block away, standing out like a drop of red ink on a blank page, is the poltergeist.

The boy stands there, scuffing one old-fashioned shoe on the sidewalk, his brown curls falling to one side as he tips his head. He is haloed with crimson light, his eyes wide and burning with the same eerie glow.

And when he looks up and sees that he has our attention, he smiles.

I swing my camera up, already hitting the flash, but he blocks his eyes, and then he turns and runs.

Not as if he's frightened, no.

As if it really is a game.

Tag.

You're it.

"Cass!" calls Jacob, but I'm already running.

The Veil ripples around me, details scrawling and erasing themselves across the paper of this place as I cut from one ghost's world into the next, Jacob on my heels.

The poltergeist is fast, too fast—he moves less like a running kid and more like a series of photos, skipping forward in time. And then, just when I think he's going to get away, the Veil flickers around us, re-forms, and suddenly, I know where we are. I've been here before.

The entrance to the Catacombs.

It looks different here, in the Veil. Older. There's no fresh green paint, no wooden door, only an iron gate. The boy, small as he is, slips through a gap between the bar and the frame, casts a final red-eyed glance back at me, and then vanishes into the dark.

I slam into the gate seconds later, but it's locked.

I pull on the bars. They rattle but don't budge. There's no way I can fit through the gap.

"We have to go after him," I say, breathless.

"No," says Jacob at my side. "That's exactly what we *don't* have to do."

I push off the gate. "You're a ghost!" I say to Jacob, waving my hand at the barricade. "Can't you just—"

"Just what?" challenges Jacob. "We're in the *Veil*. I'm as close to flesh and bone as I get. And we still don't know who that poltergeist is!"

"He tried to kill me!"

"Which, as far as I see it, is all the more reason NOT to go after him until we know enough to beat him. Lara *explicitly* told us not to engage the creepy dead child."

I glance back. "Since when do you agree with Lara?"

He holds up his hands. "I know. I'm just as surprised

as you are. And you can never *ever* tell her I said so." He gestures at the entrance to the Catacombs. "But hey, now we know something."

I turn back to the gate.

Jacob's right.

The poltergeist isn't *bound* to a Veil, isn't tied to any one moment or memory, but that doesn't mean he doesn't have one. He could have gone anywhere, but he came *here*. Why? It could be just another place to hide, but I think it's something more.

I can feel the cold pouring out through the gate, see the faint shine of red on the bars. The strange light traces the entrance like a colored pencil, as if the poltergeist and the Catacombs are made of the same stuff, stained with it. And I remember the first time I saw that eerie red glow, down in the tunnels among the bones, and I wonder if this is where it happened.

If this is where he died.

"Come on, Cass," says Jacob, reaching for my hand.

I let him take it, but not before aiming a solid kick at the iron bars. "I'm coming for you!" I shout.

You, you, you, my voice echoes into the dark. As if in

reply, a shadow crosses the Veil, and a red mist reaches through the bars like fog.

"Yeah," says Jacob, "pick a fight with the poltergeist. That's a *great* idea."

He pulls me away from the gate, and I let him.

An instant later, the gray film of the Veil disappears, and the world springs back into sudden sharpness, color, light. The sun is warm and the block is packed, throngs of tourists lining up before the green wooden shack, waiting for their turn to descend into the tombs.

Nearby, a clock begins to toll.

"Uh, Cass," says Jacob, but I'm already pulling out my phone to check the timer.

Oh *no*.

CHAPTER FOURTEEN

Trial by fire.

That's what it's called when you learn to do something under pressure.

Like navigating the Paris Metro.

I really wish I'd been paying more attention to the routes the last time we were down here. Thankfully, I dropped a pin, marking the movie theater's location on my phone, and the app tells me which Metro line to take. It's even a direct route. No need to change trains.

The journey, according to the phone, will take nineteen minutes.

The movie, according to the timer, will end in twenty-four.

Which seems like enough time until a little orange warning pops up on the screen to say the train is delayed two minutes.

Jacob counts on his fingers, frowning, and I rock back

and forth on my heels until the train finally pulls into the station, then launch myself aboard.

Nineteen minutes later, I sprint down the block and through the back door of the movie theater, down the hall and to screen number three.

I fall into the seat, knocking over the bucket of popcorn I left on the ground, and look up just in time to see the two leads kiss on a rooftop in New York as the music swells.

"Maybe one day," says Jacob as the credits begin to roll, "we can just stay and watch the movie."

Mom and Dad are waiting outside, just as they promised they would be. No sign of the crew or Pauline, who've obviously gone home for the day.

"How was the movie?" asks Mom.

"Just what I needed," I say. "How was the Rue des Chantres?"

"Oh, marvelous!" says Mom. "And marvelously haunted." She slings her arm around my shoulders. "Let's head back to the hotel. I'll tell you all about it on the way . . ."

I know something's wrong the moment we step into the hotel.

There's no icy chill, no sudden cold current, only a feeling in the air. There are too many people in the lobby, and about half of them look as if they've been caught in a storm. Which is weird, because it's been nothing but sunny since we got to Paris.

The desk clerk sees us and frowns, as if we're responsible for whatever's happened.

I shift a little. Maybe we *are*.

"What's going on?" asks Dad, approaching the counter.

The desk clerk's frown deepens. "Ah, Monsieur Blake. There has been, as you can see, an *incident*." She gestures to the damp patrons scattered across the lobby. Oh dear. "The sprinklers went off on the third floor. Most unusual. It seems the alarm was triggered from your room."

"Not it!" says Jacob quickly, holding up his hands. "Totally something I *would* do, but I didn't."

I roll my eyes. *Obviously.*

Dad shakes his head. "But we've been gone all day."

"Be that as it may," says the clerk, "*something* in your room triggered the fire alarms, and thus, the sprinklers. Perhaps," she adds, lifting something from beneath the desk, "it was *le chat noir*."

She sets Grim's cat case on the counter.

A pair of green eyes glares out, looking about as happy as the clerk as she slides the carrier toward us.

"You think our *cat* somehow triggered a fire alarm?" asks Mom.

"*Je ne sais pas,*" says the woman curtly. "What I *think* is that things *usually* run smoothly here in the Hotel Valeur . . ."

Dad's face flushes as the clerk continues. "We got your things out as quickly as possible. I assure you, they will be clean and dry in your new room. Unfortunately, as you can tell, those new rooms are not available just yet." She nods at a drinks trolley, unsmiling. "Please enjoy some coffee while you wait."

Dad starts to say something, but Mom takes his elbow in one hand and Grim's carrier in the other, and leads us to a set of chairs to wait.

"He was thinner than that," says Jacob, perched on the arm of a lobby sofa.

I'm sitting cross-legged on the marble floor, with a piece of scrap paper and one of Mom's chewed-up pencils. I've already made a list of things we know about the poltergeist, adding *Catacombs* beneath the words *short* and *young* and, on Jacob's insistence, *creepy*. Now I'm trying to put together a sketch while Jacob leans over my shoulder, offering suggestions, some helpful, and most maddening.

Dad's reading a book, while Mom raps her nails absently on the show binder with a soft *duh-duh-dum* as we wait. The other guests disappear by ones and twos as they're led to their new rooms, but we appear to be last on the list.

I force myself to focus on the drawing.

"No, his head was more like . . ." Jacob holds his hands as if gripping a basketball. Or . . . a football? A lopsided football?

"Not helpful," I mutter, erasing my first attempt, focusing instead on the boy's clothes. I wish I could thrust the pencil into Jacob's hand. Unfortunately, only one of us is real enough to hold it, so I'm left wearing eraser marks into the thin paper.

"Wouldn't it be great if you had something that could capture people's images . . . what's that called again?" Jacob is saying. "Oh yeah, A CAMERA."

I roll my eyes. My camera picks up pieces of the Veil, but

last time I checked, it didn't do a great job of accurately rendering ghosts. And even if it did, I don't exactly have a darkroom, or the time to develop a roll of film just so I can *maybe* get a photo of the creepy dead kid so I can go around asking people if they know who he was before he started haunting me.

Jacob folds his arms. "Well, when you put it *that* way . . ."

He's been in a mood ever since the mirror incident.

"Have not," he mutters. I bite my tongue, suppressing the urge to ask Jacob again about his past, his memory. But I know he hears me thinking, because he scowls and looks pointedly away.

I keep working on the sketch until I have a decent rendition of the poltergeist. A boy in tall black socks, shorts that come down to his knees, and a top that might be a shirt and might be a jacket, a wide collar clasped in front like a kerchief.

Brown curls cover the top of his round face, but something's missing.

I dig a red pen out of my bag and draw little circles around his eyes.

There.

I snap a photo with my phone and send the drawing to Lara. She texts back almost immediately.

> **Lara:**
> Did you take an art class in your American school?

> **Me:**
> No.

> **Lara:**
> I can tell.

Jacob snorts. I resist the urge to text back a snarky reply, but only because I see she's still typing.

> **Lara:**
> These clothes look like they belong to the early 20th century.

> **Lara:**
> Did you find out his name?

> **Me:**
> Not yet.

Duh-duh-dum.

I look at Mom again, the show binder under her hand, and sit up.

"Can I see that?" I ask, reaching for the binder as Mom nods. I tug it into my lap and begin turning back through the location pages, flicking past the Eiffel Tower, the Jardin du Luxembourg . . .

And then I find it: the Catacombs.

I skim the information sheet, which is mostly about the history of the tomb's construction, the different graveyards it drew from.

"Whatcha looking for?" asks Dad, leaning in as if he can *smell* research. Always the teacher, his eyes brighten at my obvious quest for information.

My mouth is already open, the word *nothing* bubbling up in that automatic way, when I stop myself.

Dad is Dad, but he's also a historian.

He's the perfect person to ask.

"When we were down in the Catacombs," I say, "you mentioned that there were people who'd gotten lost down there."

He nods gravely. "Yes, it's really no place to go wandering. Not that danger has ever stopped fools. There's an entire history of people who simply thought, 'Nothing bad will happen to *me*.'"

"Sure," I say quickly. "But do you have any of their names?"

It's a long shot, I know, more hope than certainty, but the way the red light stained that place, the way it exhaled the same strange cold, all of it felt like an extension of the boy. Like it belonged to him, or he belonged to it.

I hold my breath as I wait for Dad to answer.

"Not in there," he says, and my heart sinks a little before he adds, "But I'm sure I wrote them down."

He produces a battered leather notebook, the kind he always keeps in his back pocket. I've never been so glad my dad is such a nerd.

"Your mom and I come across a lot of stories," he says, turning through the pages. "We don't use them all in the show. Ah, here we are. There were a pair of teenage back-packers, Valerie and Michel Gillet."

He licks his thumb and turns the page.

"An older American man, George Kline. A young boy named Thomas—"

"How young?" I cut in, heart slamming in my chest.

His lips move as he does a bit of math, then says, "He would have been seven."

That's it. That's *him*. I know it, straight down to my bones.

"What did you say his name was?" I ask Dad.

"Thomas," answers Dad, pronouncing it like *Toe-MAS*. "Thomas Alain Laurent."

I turn the name over on my tongue.

"What happened to him?" I ask.

"That I don't know much about. He disappeared in 1912—snuck down into the tombs with his brother and never came out." He raises a brow. "Why the sudden curiosity?"

I hesitate. "I don't know. Ever since we went to the Catacombs, I just can't stop thinking about the people who weren't *supposed* to be buried down there."

"You sound like your father," says Mom. "Always searching for answers."

Dad beams, clearly proud to have raised a researcher. Even if the answers I'm looking for are decidedly *paranormal*. I've got plenty of my mother in me, too.

"Monsieur Blake," calls the clerk at the front desk. "Your new room is ready."

CHAPTER FIFTEEN

We gather our things—one camera, one footage briefcase, a show binder, and a very annoyed cat—and head upstairs. Our room is on the second floor this time, and as Mom unlocks the door, I send Lara an answer to her last text.

> Me:
> Thomas Alain Laurent.

The phone rings almost instantly.

"Impressive," says Lara. I can hear her fingers tapping on a keyboard. "That's definitely a start."

I hang back in the hall. "A start? I know his *name*."

"He's not Rumpelstiltskin," says Lara. "A name doesn't mean much without the memories that go with it."

I slump back against the wallpaper. "I miss the days when all I had to do was hold up a mirror."

"Nonsense," says Lara. "Who doesn't love a good challenge?"

"Easy for you to say," I reply. "So far I've been pushed off a roof, nearly crushed by a set piece, and narrowly avoided being hit by a giant mirror. Not to mention, he flooded our room at the hotel."

"You've had quite a day."

"Yeah, I think it's safe to say we've moved past mischief." I lower my voice. "I'm worried, Lara. About my parents. About myself. Worried he'll catch me off guard. Worried about what he'll do before I can face him."

"Yes, about that," says Lara, "it sounds as though you could use some protection. Uncle Weathershire says you can use sage and salt to ward off strong spirits."

"Where am I supposed to get sage and salt?" I ask.

"Lucky for you, you have me."

"And as grateful as I am," I say, "you are in another country."

"Didn't you get my package?"

"What?" I finally walk into the hotel room, and see a small brown parcel, roughly the size and shape of a book, wrapped with black ribbon. Unfortunately, Mom notices it, too. She picks it up, reads the label, and stares at me.

"Cassidy Blake, did you *order* something off the internet?"

"It's from Lara," I say, swiping the parcel from her hands.

I retreat to the bedroom and examine the box. A folded slip on top reads: *For Cassidy Blake, with compliments.*

"After we spoke yesterday," continues Lara, "I made some calls. Uncle has—well, *had*—a number of contacts throughout the paranormal world, including a couple there in Paris. Lovely people."

I turn the card over. On the back, it's signed: *La Société du Chat Noir.*

I remember the desk clerk calling Grim a *chat noir.*

"The Society of the Black Cat," Lara translates for me. "Fascinating group, very eclectic, and, of course, quite secret. They have chapters in most major cities, but you need to know someone who knows someone . . ."

I study the card. First poltergeists, now secret societies? I'm starting to realize how little I know about the paranormal world beyond my parents' show and my own experiences in the Veil.

"And you're a member of this society?" I ask, setting the card aside.

"Not yet," says Lara, sounding annoyed. "They have a rather stringent age restriction. But I'm petitioning for a special exemption."

"Of course you are," mutters Jacob.

I open the box, and he immediately begins to sneeze.

"Oh, yes," says Lara, "I should have mentioned. Sage and salt works on *all* ghosts."

"You totally—*achoo*—knew—*achoo*—this would—*achoo*—happen."

I slam the box shut.

Jacob glowers, sniffling.

"Thanks, Lara," I say.

"Yeah," grumbles Jacob, retreating to the open window. "Thanks."

That night, I slip pouches of sage and salt into Dad's jacket and Mom's purse, hoping those will be enough to keep the poltergeist away.

From my parents, at least.

The sachets also seem to be working on Jacob.

He usually waits to leave until I'm ready for bed, but

there's been no sign of him since dinner. He said he was going to patrol the hotel for Thomas. But I suspect he's looking for residents to scare. Then again, maybe he just wants to get away from the extra herbs I've sprinkled on the windows and outside the door, because the thought of Thomas slipping in at night is more than I can handle.

And even with the sachets, I can't sleep.

Finally, I throw off the covers and open the window, leaning out on the iron rail. The breeze is cool, the Veil whispering against my skin. I draw the pendant from beneath my collar, let the mirror spin on its chain between my fingers, my reflection there and gone, there and gone.

A mirror shows us what we know.

I think of Jacob, of his face as he stood over the shattered mirror today, the way he pulled free of his reflection.

A poltergeist is what happens when a ghost forgets.

I close my eyes, arms crossed on the rail.

Jacob must have gotten lucky. He must have not really been looking.

He's not forgetting, I tell myself.

He's not forgetting.

I can feel my head drooping.

He's not . . .

A car alarm goes off a couple of streets away. I jerk upright, my heart slamming in my chest, as another goes off, then another, as if someone is banging on every hood.

"Thomas Alain Laurent."

I say the name into the dark, as if the words might summon him, but there's nothing there. I look down at the street below, half expecting to see a little boy looking back. But the street stays empty.

And yet.

Something steals through me like a chill.

And I hear it, soft as whispers on the wind.

"Un . . . deux . . . trois . . ."

I don't know what makes me reach for my camera—maybe a hunch, or the faint memory of how, once, it let me see through the Veil itself—but as I bring the viewfinder to my eye and adjust the focus, the night beyond, and the street below, begins to shift and blur.

". . . quatre . . . cinq . . . six . . ."

And there he is.

Thomas Alain Laurent stands on the street, his head tipped back toward the open window, his edges rippling, his eyes bright and hollow and red, and leveled on me. I snap a photo, no flash. Crank the film. Snap again. As if I'm afraid he'll disappear again between shots.

He stops counting and holds out his hand, an invitation to come out and play.

He flashes me a trickster's grin, but when I shake my head, his face falls, dropping from a smile into a child's sneer. The effect is so sudden and eerie that I pull the view-finder away from my eye. Without it, the street below looks empty again.

And when I get up the courage to lift the camera and look again, Thomas is gone.

CHAPTER SIXTEEN

The floor trembles and the walls shake, as if the whole hotel is shivering.

I'm crouched on the floor behind a pillar, trying to avoid the debris as it flies across the lobby.

"Jacob, listen to me!" I call out over the sound of rattling picture frames and breaking glass.

He's curled in on himself in the center of the marble floor, the air around him whipped into a frenzy.

"*Stop,*" he pleads as water runs from his clothes, dripping onto the marble floor. His hair floats around his face, which is ashen, gray.

"Cassidy!" orders Lara from behind the front desk. "You have to send him on."

No. I can still save him.

I grip my camera, take a deep breath, and lunge out from the shelter of the pillar, already turning the lens on Jacob.

I hit the flash, hoping the burst of light will jar him loose, bring him back to his senses. But the function on the camera jams, and before I can try again, a violent gust snaps the strap and rips the camera from my hands. It slams into the far wall with a sickening crunch. No, no, no.

A gust of wind shoves me backward, and I struggle to stay on my feet.

"Jacob!" I shout as the ceiling cracks and splits, raining down dust.

The hotel shakes around us, as if it's about to come down.

"Stop," Jacob says, finally lifting his head. "Stop me."

And when looks at me, his eyes are glowing, no longer blue but *red*.

I sit up with a lurch, my heart racing.

Sunlight streams in through the curtains, and through Jacob, who's perched cross-legged at the end of my bed.

"You should see your hair, Cass." He runs his hands through his own, making it stand on end.

"You know it's super creepy," I say, "when you watch me sleep."

Jacob hops up, leaving the barest mark on the comforter. "I wasn't watching you sleep. I was trying to wake you up." He points at the phone on my bedside table. "It was going off. Lara kept calling." He pokes the cell, his fingers going straight through the screen. "Trust me, if I could hang up on her, I would."

I scramble up and grab the phone, scrolling through the texts.

Lara:
I found something—or rather someone.

Lara:
Call me.

Lara:
It's important.

"Who uses proper punctuation in a text?" says Jacob.

"Uh-huh," I say half-heartedly, still shaken from the dream.

"You okay?" he asks, eyeing me. "You seem . . . off."

"I'm fine," I answer quickly, my stomach dropping even as I say the words. Second rule of friendship: No lies.

I hit CALL.

"*Finally,*" says Lara.

"Do you ever sleep?" I ask, rubbing my eyes.

"I get the requisite seven to eight hours," says Lara, "though I confess I've always functioned better on seven."

"Cass!" calls Mom, rapping her knuckles on the door even though it's ajar. "We're heading down to the salon for breakfast. You ready?"

I put my hand over the phone. "I'll meet you there!" I call back. "I need a few more minutes."

"Don't go back to sleep!" warns Dad.

"I won't."

It took me ages to fall asleep last night after the Thomas sighting, and between that and the dream, I feel wide-awake.

"What dream?" asks Jacob, reading my thoughts.

I shake my head, pushing the nightmare to the back of my mind.

"And you saw the creepy kid?" he presses.

"Hello?" says Lara. "Earth to Cassidy."

"Sorry," I say, turning my attention back to the phone. "What were you saying?"

"Only that I have a lead for you. You're very welcome."

"You're supposed to say that *after* I say thanks. What's the lead?"

"Okay, so the bad news is that there's no information on Thomas Alain Laurent, besides what you already know."

"Talk about a literal dead end," muses Jacob.

"Yes," says Lara, "but not really a surprise. He did die a hundred years before the invention of the internet. *But* I found something. Thomas's older brother, Richard."

My heart does a flip. "He's still *alive*?"

"Don't be ridiculous," says Lara. "But he *did* stay in Paris. Now, French names have far less variance than, say, American ones—there are a thousand Laurents— but thankfully Thomas and Richard's parents had pretty unusual *prénoms*; that means first names—"

"Can we fast-forward?" I ask, desperate for a lead.

"Fine," snaps Lara. "I'm pretty sure I found them. Your Laurents. Richard died thirty years ago, at the ripe old age of eighty-nine, but his granddaughter, Sylvaine, still lives in the city. I'm texting you her address. Maybe she knows the full story. Maybe she even has something that can help jog Thomas's memory."

"Lara," I say. "You are amazing."

"I know," she says, "but this wasn't terribly difficult. You'd be surprised what you can find if you know how to look. My school teaches fairly rigorous research methods."

"Is there anything your school *doesn't* teach?"

"Apparently how to hunt a poltergeist."

Jacob makes a gasping sound. "Lara Chowdhury, did you just make a *joke*?"

I can almost hear Lara smile. *"Anyway,"* she says. "Good luck. And be careful."

"You don't have to say that every time."

"You'd think not," she says. "And yet."

The call ends, the screen replaced by Lara's text bubble with the address of a Madame Sylvaine Laurent in the eleventh arrondissement.

I have a lead.

Now I just have to convince my parents to let me follow it.

We're having breakfast down in the salon when I bring it up, and in the end, it's easier than I expected.

Dad preens when I tell him about a break in the case, clearly excited to have a budding sleuth in the family. But Mom, for once, seems wary.

"Where's this sudden interest coming from?"

I look down at my croissant.

"Well," I say, "I know you asked me to take photos for the show, but I also started thinking about the people whose stories *don't* make the show. I wanted to learn more about them, and something about this Thomas boy just stuck with me. I can't shake the feeling there's more to his story," I finish, hoping it doesn't *sound* like I practiced that in the mirror. Several times.

"I'm sure it's a very interesting tale, Cass," says Mom, "and good on you for digging deeper. But our schedule here is so tight. It's our last day to film and—"

"I can take her."

The words come from Pauline, of all people.

"We can't ask you to do that," says Dad, but Pauline flicks her hand dismissively.

"It is no trouble," she says. "You two will be fine with Anton and Annette. They know this city as well as I do.

Besides, Cassidy has been very patient, and this mission clearly means a lot to her." She glances my way, eyebrows raised, clearly prompting me to emphasize.

"It does!" I say.

Mom and Dad exchange a long look, and then agree, on the strict rules that I won't bother the Laurents if they don't want to be bothered, and that I'll come back to the hotel as soon as it's done.

"You'll miss the Butcher of Marmousets," says Mom with a sigh.

"Don't even think about asking what that is," warns Jacob.

I swing my camera bag onto my shoulder and hug my parents, patting the pocket of Dad's tweed coat to make sure the pouch of sage and salt is safe inside.

And then we're off.

"Why did you offer to go with me?" I ask Pauline as we get on the Metro.

"You are a child," she says, "and Paris is a big city. It's not safe to go wandering alone."

I want to point out that I'm neither a *child* nor *alone*,

and I've actually already gone exploring. But then again, that nearly ended in death by mirror, so maybe she's onto something. Besides, now I have a translator.

I rock on my heels. "It wouldn't have anything to do with the fact my parents are going to that *butcher* place today, would it?"

"Nonsense," she says, a little too quickly.

"You're not scared, are you?" I ask. "I mean, you don't believe in any of these things."

"Exactly."

The train murmurs softly as it moves beneath Paris. It's warm and crowded, a motley collection of people, some in suits, and others in jogging gear, high heels mixed in with rainbow flats. Most of them are on their phones, but a handful read paperbacks or newspapers or stare into space.

The train rocks a little as it gains speed.

Jacob stares out the window at the darkness sailing past the glass, and the effect is chilling, his reflection little more than streaks and blurs. An image submerged, dissolving. I think of the nightmare, and then do everything I can *not* to think of it. I end up focusing instead on Thomas Laurent.

The fact I haven't seen him since last night.

Somehow, I don't find that very comforting.

I thumb the camera absently, and Pauline nods toward it. "That's quite an interesting model."

You have no idea, I think, running my fingers over the battered metal casing. "It's old and quirky, but I like it."

"My father is a photographer," she says. "He restores old cameras. He says they see better than new ones."

I smile. "Yeah, they really do."

"If you like," she offers, "my father could develop your film."

I look up and smile. "Really? That would be great." I consider the canister of film. "I miss my darkroom," I confess. That closet of space back home that was mine, and mine alone.

Jacob clears his throat.

Well, ours.

"Perhaps," says Pauline, "you could even—"

But I don't hear the rest.

A cold wind rushes over my skin, and Pauline's words are drowned out by the grinding of metal on rails.

The train screeches, as if someone's tapped the brakes a little too hard, and I nearly lose my balance. I shift my grip on the metal bar just in time. The train brakes again, and grinds to a stop on the darkened rail.

Oh great, I think, right before all the lights go out.

PART FOUR

MAYHEM

CHAPTER SEVENTEEN

I t's not pitch-black.

Thin light leaks through the windows from somewhere far down the tunnel, painting all the passengers in a weak glow. Everyone begins to grumble and look around, more annoyed than afraid. But Pauline's hand goes straight to the charm at her throat, and even in the almost-dark I can see her lips moving.

Jacob moves closer to me, his gaze flicking my way.

In the dark, he looks almost solid, just another body in the crowded car.

"Thomas?" he asks, and I nod. I lift the camera's viewfinder to one eye, slide the darkened train in and out of focus, searching the crowd for a little boy who isn't there.

"Maybe this isn't him," says Jacob, sounding a little unconvinced. "I mean, trains stop running sometimes, don't they? Technical malfunctions, power to the third rail . . . I don't know what the third rail is, exactly, but I've heard people say that . . ."

Sure, I think, lowering the camera. *And sometimes massive mirrors fall off trucks . . .*

I take a step forward, then stop. I should stay put, stay here, firmly on the real side of life.

"I completely agree," says Jacob. "Do not engage the poltergeist."

After all, there's nothing I can do until I know his story, know enough to remind him.

"Do not engage," repeats Jacob.

But then I see it through the camera lens—a curl of red light against the far window.

"Do not engage," warns Jacob as I feel myself reaching for the Veil.

I have his name now. His *full* name. It was enough to call him to the street last night. Maybe it will be enough to catch him here. Enough to make him remember.

Pauline has her back to us, scanning the car, and I step sideways, into the dark.

The crush of water in my lungs and then—

I'm back in the Veil.

I expected to find a stretch of bare gray space: an absence, a gap between places, the spaces where no ghosts have met their ends.

So I'm unnerved when my foot comes down on solid steel.

The car is empty, the crowd erased, but the train car is here, drawn in crisp, clear lines, the kind that only come with someone else's memory. A ghost's memory.

Jacob appears beside me.

"What part of do not engage . . ." he says, trailing off as the lights flicker in and out around us, illuminating empty benches. Bare floor. No sign of a little boy in old-fashioned clothes. No crop of dark curls or glowing red eyes. But I know he's here.

"Thomas?" I call out, but the word only echoes. *Thomas, Thomas, Thomas.* "Thomas Alain Laurent?"

I go to the end of the train car and slide the latch. The door springs open, and I cross into the next car, expecting to find it empty.

It's not.

No Thomas, but a tall man stands in the center of the car, his back to us, swaying on his feet. Something dark and red stains the floor beneath his boots. He mumbles softly to himself, not in French, but in English.

"Who did it?" he growls, twisting toward us. "Who did it?"

And as he turns, I see the knife buried in his stomach. His own hand curled around the blade as if to keep it from falling out. The sheen of blood running down his front. "Who did it?" he growls again, taking a staggering step toward us. "Was it *you*?"

Jacob pulls me backward and slams the door between us.

"Well, *that's* going to haunt my dreams," he says as we straddle the space between the cars. "As fun as this was—"

"*Un, deux, trois . . .*" calls a playful voice behind me. A familiar voice. Thomas.

The voice is coming from the front of the train. Along with an eerie red glow.

I step down from the train onto the tracks, squinting down the line of cars.

"Thomas Alain Laurent!" I shout. "Come out, come out, wherever you are."

The red light dances along the tunnel wall, and I can hear the shuffle of small feet. A soft giggle. I clutch the pendant as I creep down the side of the train car.

But he doesn't show himself.

Maybe Lara was right; maybe the name isn't enough.

"Thomas, please," I call, and then, mustering my only French, *"S'il vous plaît."*

The red light brightens, shining along the tracks, and I see a pair of red eyes peek between cars. I hold out my hand, the way Thomas did on the street last night, an invitation to come play.

Thomas smiles.

And then he presses his small hands to the side of the train. The crimson light ripples out from his fingers, and then he giggles again, and *disappears*.

"No," I hiss, jerking forward, but Jacob grabs my arm.

"Cass."

"What?" I snap, twisting free.

"The train."

And I don't understand what he means until I hear it.

A faint and far-off groan. The sound isn't human.

It's *metal*.

And it's coming from the other side of the Veil. The power is back on. The train is starting up again.

I lurch toward the gap between cars as the ghostly train creeps forward. Jacob gets there first, hauls himself up, and offers a hand, and I'm grateful that he's solid enough for me to take it.

He pulls me up just as the train begins to gain speed, and I throw open the door, and the Veil with it, stepping back into the real world as the lights flicker on around us.

Pauline sees me through the crowd and frowns as I weave my way toward her.

"There you are," she says, grabbing my shoulder.

Her eyes are wide, her face pale, her other hand clutching the pendant at her chest. And I realize it's the first time I've seen her truly lose her composure. The first time I've seen her mask of calm slip, reveal the thing beneath: fear.

Pauline is terrified.

"You're *not* a skeptic, are you?" I say.

She lets go of my shoulder and forces out a steadying breath. "I don't know what you're talking about."

I narrow my eyes. "You're not just superstitious. You're a *believer*."

Pauline bristles. "No, of course not."

But the *no* is too quick, too forceful.

"What are you ashamed of?" I ask. "You're with a group of people whose whole job is to believe in ghosts."

"I'm not *ashamed* of anything," she retorts, folding her arms across her chest. "I don't *want* to believe in ghosts."

"But you do."

She sighs. Hesitates. "What was it you said? It is easy not to believe, and then once you experience something, it's hard not to?"

The train pulls into the station.

"I have . . . seen things, once or twice. Things I could not explain." Pauline shakes her head as the doors slide open. "*Mon dieu*, I sound like a fool."

I shrug. "Not to me." She manages a small, tight-lipped smile, then shoos me off the train onto the platform.

It seems busy, even busier than usual. People are muttering under their breaths and clustering in front of electronic signs that show the different Metro lines, red warnings popping up beside them. First one, then two, then four.

"What's going on?" I ask.

"It looks like our train is not the only one having trouble," says Pauline.

"There's no way Thomas could be doing all *that*," says Jacob. He looks at me, a little nervous. "Right?"

I want to believe him. But I don't. The warnings flash, bright red, and all I can see are the poltergeist's eyes, the way the crimson seemed to spread out into the air around him.

First comes mischief, then comes menace, then mayhem.

The more trouble poltergeists cause, the more powerful they get.

We have to hurry.

I turn to Pauline, holding out the address for Sylvaine Laurent. "Lead the way."

"Tell me, Cassidy," says Pauline as we walk. "Why are you so interested in this family?"

"Mom says I've always been naturally curious."

She raises a brow. "Is that all? Or is there another reason you wish to visit the Laurents?"

I shift my weight from foot to foot. "Do you really want to know?"

Pauline seems to genuinely consider it. "No, I think

not," she says, then sighs. "But you should probably tell me anyway."

So, I do.

I tell her about ghosts and poltergeists, about the fact that I somehow woke one poltergeist up and now it's following me, causing all kinds of trouble.

Pauline blinks, her hand drifting to the charm around her neck. "And the Laurents . . . ?"

"They're the poltergeist's family," I say. "I'm hoping if I learn what really happened to Thomas, it will help me send him on."

Pauline starts to speak, but an emergency vehicle whips past, sirens wailing. She waits for them to fade, then starts again.

"And why is it *your* job to send this spirit on?"

"That's a great question!" says Jacob, but I ignore him.

"I guess because I can. A year or so ago, I almost died, and now I can cross the Veil—that's the place between this world and the one with the ghosts—and my friend Lara says it's kind of like paying back a debt."

"That seems like a lot of pressure for a girl so young."

"Oh, I don't have to do it alone," I say. "I have Jacob."

She raises a brow. "Jacob?"

"He's my best friend," I say, adding, "He's a ghost."

This time both eyebrows go up. "I see." And despite what she just said about believing, I can tell she doesn't believe *me*.

When I tell her that, she sighs. "I believe that *you* believe."

I shake my head. "Why is it that when kids believe in something, adults write it off as imagination, but when adults believe in something, people assume it's true?"

"I'm not sure anyone would assume *this* is true."

"But you just said you've seen things. You said you believed."

Pauline shakes her head. "Belief is not a blanket, Cassidy. It doesn't cover everything. Forgive me. There's a big difference between believing in the supernatural in the general sense and believing the twelve-year-old girl you're escorting across Paris is a ghost hunter with a dead sidekick."

"Excuse *me*," says Jacob. "Who is she calling *sidekick*?"

Before I can explain that he's more of a partner in crime, Pauline stops, gesturing to a lemon-yellow building with white accents and flower baskets in the windows. "Here we are."

It's an old-fashioned apartment building. Lara didn't give me an apartment number, but a quick scan of the buzzers running down the right side says that "Mme Laurent" lives in 3A. A man is walking out of the building, and I catch the front door before it can swing closed behind him. Pauline and I slip inside.

We're climbing the stairs when my nerves finally catch up.

What I'm doing is ridiculous; it's insane.

"Agreed," says Jacob.

I'm hoping Lara's knack for investigation paid off and that I'm even in the right place.

But it's also the only lead I have.

I reach 3A, and my hand hesitates over the wood for a long second before I swallow, and knock.

A few moments later, a girl answers the door.

She's maybe a year or two younger than me, in gold sneakers, jeans, and a pink-and-white sweater. Her skin is fair and her light brown hair is pulled up in a high ponytail, glossy and straight (I have no idea how people get hair like that—mine's always been wild). The white stem of a lollipop sticks out the side of her mouth.

"*Bonjour?*" she says, tipping her chin.

I glance over my shoulder at Pauline, but she says nothing, just stands there unhelpfully, so I turn back.

"Hi," I reply in English. "Um, *parlez-vous anglais?*" I ask, mustering some French (and definitely butchering it).

The girl considers me, then nods.

"Yes," she says proudly, "I go to an international school, and they make us learn. It is a . . . clunky language, *n'est-ce pas?*"

"Sure," I say, just glad she speaks it. "Are you Sylvaine Laurent?"

She draws back a little. "*Mais non,*" she says with a nervous laugh. "I am Adele. Sylvaine is my mother." She calls back into the apartment, "*Maman!*" and then slips away without so much as a goodbye.

A moment later, a woman appears, wiping her hands on a dish towel. She looks like Adele, only older, her light brown hair hanging loose down to her shoulders. She even tilts her head the same way as she comes to the door.

"*Oui?*" she asks, addressing Pauline.

But Pauline shakes her head. *"C'est pas moi,"* she says, nodding at me. So I guess I'm on my own here. Sylvaine Laurent stares down at me, a wary look in her eyes.

"Hi, Madame Laurent," I say, trying to muster Mom's easy smile, or Dad's confidence. "I'm researching a story about your great-uncle, Thomas Laurent."

Sylvaine frowns a little. "What kind of story?"

"Well," I say, faltering, "um, I guess it's a *research* story?"

"This is going smoothly," says Jacob, rocking on his heels.

"How did you hear about Thomas?" presses Sylvaine. For a second, I'm just glad she knows who I'm talking about, but the excitement wears off when her frown becomes an outright scowl.

"Oh, right." I swallow, wishing I were a little older, or at least a little taller. "Well, my parents are hosting a television show about ghosts in Paris, and we were down in the Catacombs, and I heard—"

But Madame Laurent is already shaking her head.

"What happened to Thomas happened a long time ago," she says, her tone cold. "It is not fit for speaking."

I look to Pauline, silently begging her to say something, to intercede, but she only shrugs.

The girl, Adele, reappears in the foyer, lingering behind her mother, clearly curious.

"Please, Madame Laurent," I try again. "I just want to help—"

She doesn't give me a chance to finish, turning her attention to Pauline. They exchange a few words in rapid French, and then our Paris guide brings her hand to my shoulder.

"Come, Cassidy," Pauline says. "We must return to your parents."

"But I need to know—"

"*Non*," says Madame Laurent, her face flushing pink. "You do not. History is history. It is past. And *private*."

And with that she shuts the door in my face.

CHAPTER EIGHTEEN

I sag back against the landing in defeat.

One step forward, two steps back, and zero steps closer to sending Thomas on.

"You tried," says Pauline. "It did not work. These things happen." She tugs a slip of paper from her pocket. A schedule. "Your parents should be on their way to the Pont Marie. We can meet them there—"

"You *knew* she wouldn't talk to me."

Pauline shrugs again. "I suspected, perhaps. The French are private people."

"But you didn't say anything!" I cry, exasperated. "You let me come all this way. Why didn't you warn me?"

Pauline turns her sharp eyes on me. "Would it have stopped you?"

I open my mouth to protest, then close it again.

"That's what I thought."

I want to shout, to say that it *has* to work. That Thomas is getting stronger, and I have to learn his story so I can remind him who he is, so that the mirror will work and I can send him on before someone gets *hurt*, or worse.

Instead, I press my palms against my eyes to clear my head and follow Pauline down the stairs and out into the sun.

We walk to the bridge in silence, the trip punctuated only by the occasional siren, an emergency vehicle rushing past. I tell myself it's not Thomas. I hope it's not Thomas.

"The upside," observes Jacob, "is that if it *is* Thomas, it seems like he's no longer fixated on *you*."

Somehow, that doesn't make me feel better.

Jacob glances over his shoulder, frowns.

What is it? I ask silently.

He hesitates, then shakes his head. "Nothing."

The Seine comes into sight, and I spy my parents leaning against the stone lip of a bridge, waiting while Anton and Annette adjust their cameras.

Paris has a ton of bridges crisscrossing the river and running from the banks to the two islands that float in the middle. This particular bridge doesn't look all that special—it's the same pale stone as so much of the city—but as my shoes hit the edge, the Veil pulses, rippling around me. Jacob shoots me a warning look, and I force the Veil back, manage to keep my feet.

By the time Pauline and I reach Mom and Dad, they've already started filming.

"Paris has many ghost stories," begins Mom. "Some of them scary and some of them strange, some of them gruesome and some simply sad. But few are as tragic as the ghost of the Pont Marie."

Jacob looks over his shoulder again, and I assume he's just keeping an eye out for Thomas.

"During World War Two," explains Dad, "the Resistance relied on spies to steal information, smuggle secrets from the Nazi forces."

"Hey, Cass," says Jacob, but I shush him.

"It's said that the wife of a Resistance fighter became a spy in an unconventional way. She began seeing a Nazi soldier and took his secrets back to her husband. The woman and her husband would meet here, on the Pont Marie, at midnight . . ."

"*Cass,*" whispers Jacob again.

"What is it?" I hiss.

"Someone's following us."

What?

I turn to follow Jacob's gaze, already lifting the camera viewfinder to my eye. I brace myself, expecting to see Thomas. But instead I see a girl with a high ponytail and gold sneakers that catch the light.

Adele.

To her credit, she doesn't try to blend in or hide. She doesn't even pretend to be looking at anyone or anything else. She just stands at the edge of the bridge, arms folded and head cocked, the white lollipop stick still in her mouth.

"But one cold winter night," continues Mom, "the woman came to the bridge, and her husband did not. He never showed, and she froze to death right here, secrets frozen on her tongue . . ."

I walk up to Adele.

She's a good head shorter than me, but she stares up, unblinking.

"How long have you been following me?" I ask her.

She shrugs. "Since you left our house."

"Why?"

"I heard what you said to my mother." Her eyes narrow. "Why are you *really* interested in Thomas Laurent?"

"I told your mom—I'm researching a story."

"Why?"

"For school," I lie.

"It's summer."

"Fine," I say. "I just want to know."

"Why?"

"I'm curious."

"Why?"

I let out an exasperated breath. "Because I'm a ghost hunter, and Thomas Laurent is a ghost. Actually, he's a poltergeist, which is like a ghost but stronger. I accidentally woke him up or something, and now he's causing all kinds of problems, and I have to send him on to the other side, but I can't do that until I figure out who he is—was—because he doesn't remember."

Jacob puts his head in his hands and groans, but Adele simply stares at me, chewing the inside of her cheek, and I wonder if the language barrier ate up half my words.

But then, after a long moment, she nods.

"Okay."

"Okay?"

"I believe you."

She has a small backpack slung over one shoulder, and as I watch, she unzips it and pulls out a dozen cards, their edges fraying. "I brought you these," she says, holding them out so I can see. They're *photographs*, black and white, and faded with age.

One of the photographs is of a boy. I recognize Thomas instantly.

The round face, the wild curls, the smile. Not menacing here, but open, cheerful. Something rattles through me at the sight of this boy, not faded but solid, bright-eyed, alive.

Real.

I take the photos, turning through the stack. In the next one, Thomas isn't alone. A boy, several years older than him, stands beside him, one hand resting playfully on the younger boy's head. That must be . . .

"That's Richard," says Adele. "Thomas's older brother. My great-grandfather."

The third photo is a family portrait, the two boys side by side, framed by their parents, who stand stiff-backed and straight. And in the last photo, the older boy, Richard, stands alone in front of a Parisian building, his eyes a little sad. I recognize the doorway, the arch of the windows. I was just there. The building where the Laurents still live.

"Do these photos help you?" asks Adele.

I nod. "Thank you."

It's not Thomas's story, but it's something. After all, photos are memories pressed into paper. Maybe showing them to Thomas will jog his memory. But in order for that to work, I have to *find* him again.

"Cass!" calls Mom as she and Dad walk over, the crew on their heels.

Jacob sniffles a little and retreats, repelled by the sage-and-salt pouches I planted in their pockets and bags. "We're done here. How was your adventure? And who's this charming girl?"

"Adele Laurent," she answers before I can. "I am helping Cassidy with her"—and I have to resist the urge to throw my hand over her mouth before she finishes—"research project."

Pauline looks surprised, but Mom only beams. "How nice!"

"That's wonderful," adds Dad.

"Yeah, she's been super helpful," I say.

I'm about to offer to walk the girl home, a perfect opportunity to slip away and maybe learn more about Thomas, but Adele says, "You are filming a show about ghosts, *n'est pas?*"

"That's right," says Dad. "We're on our way to our next location. Our last one, actually."

Adele brightens. And then, before I can get a word in, she adds, "Cassidy said I could come with you."

I most certainly did not.

"Of course," says Mom. "If it's all right with your parents?"

Adele shrugs. "*Maman* doesn't mind where I go, so long as I'm careful."

Lucky, I think.

"Well," adds Dad, gesturing across the bridge to an island, where a cathedral rises against the skyline. "All we have left to film is Notre-Dame."

"*C'est cool!*" says Adele.

As soon as my parents turn to go, I round on the girl. "I didn't say that you could come."

She shrugs. "I know, but it's summer. There's nothing to

do. And this sounds *much* more fun than watching television. Besides, you owe me. I helped you."

"Yeah, you did," I say. "And, look, thanks for the photos, but it's not safe, and you need to go home."

"I can help you more," she counters stubbornly. "I speak French, and I fit into small places—"

"Adele—"

"Plus, he is *my* family, not yours."

"Girls!" calls Mom over her shoulder. "Are you coming?"

Adele smiles, and jogs to catch up.

And somehow, just like that, I've gained a shadow.

CHAPTER NINETEEN

We weave through the streets, the twin stone towers of Notre-Dame rising ahead of us.

As we walk, I turn through the old photos again, searching for clues. I keep coming back to the one with the two brothers. They're both smiling, and Richard has one hand planted in the mop of Thomas's hair. Before, I was focused on Thomas, but this time, I can't stop looking at Richard. His hair is lighter than Thomas's, tucked beneath a cap, his face leaner and more angled, but it's his eyes that stop me. They're happy, bright, and they remind me of someone.

"He kind of looks like you," I whisper, tipping the photo toward Jacob. A shadow crosses Jacob's face, and for an instant he looks distracted, sad.

"I don't see it," he mumbles, looking away.

"Who are you talking to?" asks Adele, bobbing along beside me.

"Jacob. He's a ghost."

She crinkles her nose. "But I thought you hunted ghosts."

Jacob and I exchange a look.

"I do," I say. For a terrible second, the nightmare rises up in my mind, and I push it down. "But Jacob's different."

A breeze blows through, sudden and cold, and I'm already tensing, looking for Thomas, but Adele seems to feel it, too. She crosses her arms, scrunching up her shoulders.

"Have you noticed," she says, "it's getting colder?"

"That can't be good," says Jacob, and I don't know if he means the falling temperature or the fact the cold is now strong enough for someone normal to feel, but either way, I agree.

I start walking faster. We catch up with my parents and the crew at an intersection, waiting for the crosswalk light to turn green. The chill is still hanging on the air, and I look around, sure that something is about to go wrong. But it doesn't, and I'm starting to wonder if it's just weather when the light turns green and I step off the curb into the street.

I make it one step, two, and then I hear the screech of tires, the wail of a horn.

I look up too late. See the car too late. Jacob is twisting toward me, but it's Dad who grabs my shoulder and wrenches me back out of the street. An instant later, the car plows by, blaring its horn, and I'm left gasping and shaking on the curb.

"Cassidy!" snaps Dad. "What were you thinking?"

"But the light—" I start, looking up toward the crosswalk light. Sure enough, it's green. But so is *every* stoplight. Horns blast and cars screech to a stop, the intersection losing all composure.

"It must be a glitch," says Mom, pulling me close.

"Yeah," I say, teeth chattering with cold. "Must be."

Jacob's right about one thing.

Thomas isn't my problem anymore.

He's *everyone's*.

Ten minutes later, we're climbing one of Notre-Dame's towers.

The cathedral has given us a thirty-minute window to film, clearing the tourists ahead and delaying the ones behind, so we're alone on the tight spiral stairs. Just the crew, Mom and Dad, Pauline, me, and Jacob—and Adele, practically skipping up the steps. I pull my sweater tight. It might just be the drafty stone staircase, but I can't seem to shake the chill.

"Thousands flock to Notre-Dame to see its sculpted doorways and stained glass," Dad narrates to the camera.

"But this medieval cathedral," Mom steps in, "is home to as many ghost stories as gargoyles."

"But why are there so many *stairs*?" asks Jacob as we climb.

Says the one who doesn't have to take them.

Jacob looks at me for a second, eyes wide. "Oh yeah," he says, scratching his head. "I forgot."

I roll my eyes, and he salutes.

"See you corporeal kids at the top," he says, vanishing upward through the ceiling.

Adele plucks the white stick from her mouth, the lollipop gone, and pockets the bare stem. She produces two more lollipops from her bag and hands one to me. I take it, even though my stomach is in knots.

"How do you know," she asks, "if a place is haunted?"

"I can feel it," I say softly. "The world gets ... heavier, and when a ghost is nearby, it feels like this." I reach out and rap my finger on her shoulder. *Tap-tap-tap.*

Back home, where things were decidedly less haunted, the tapping would usually come out of nowhere, hitting me like a clap of thunder. But it's been a steady beat since we started our trip. Sometimes the tapping is faint and sometimes it is strong, but these cities are so haunted, I'm more likely to notice when there *isn't* a spectral presence.

Adele smiles. "Cool." And then, "Can you teach me how to know?"

I shake my head. "No, sorry. It's not something you can really learn."

She frowns, confused, and I explain, "It only works if you've almost died."

Her eyes widen, and I can tell she's about to ask a million more questions, but we reach the first landing and I cut her off. "We have to be quiet while they're filming."

We step out onto a stone balcony dotted with stone monsters. A metal cage arches over our heads, a barrier between us and the ledge. I hang back, but Adele reaches through the grate to brush her fingers over a gargoyle's foot.

Mom runs her hand along the metal mesh. "These barricades," she says, "are not for show. Some have fallen. Others have jumped. A few might even have been pushed. Take a young woman, for example, known only as M. J. She wished to climb up here but needed a chaperone, and so she befriended an old woman, and together, the two ascended the tower." Mom's expression darkens. "No one knows what happened next. The young woman's body was found on the stones below. The old lady was never seen again."

I shudder a little, feeling that *tap-tap-tap*. But Adele's eyes have gone bright with delight at Mom's words. As if these are all just stories, held back from reality, the way we are held back from the balcony's edge.

Jacob's standing at the corner, peering out at the city, a dark expression on his face. I cross to him and follow his gaze, my breath catching in my chest at the sight of Paris below.

It's not just the view.

It's the sound of sirens, high as a whistle.

The red-and-blue lights winking across the skyline.

The tendril of smoke rising from a building in the distance.

The chill that's hanging in the air, as if it's fall instead of the middle of the summer.

Thomas Alain Laurent has officially made his way to mayhem.

Mom and Dad and the crew move along, vanishing into the bell tower at the other end of the balcony. Adele follows them, but I hang back, looking through the protective mesh. We're a long way up. Which means it's a long way down.

An idea forms in the back of my mind.

A look of horror sweeps across Jacob's face.

"Cassidy, wait—"

But I'm already cutting through the Veil.

That short, sharp drop, through black water and into gray, and then I'm back on the cathedral balcony, bells tolling, the two towers rising into fog overhead.

There is really only one difference: Here in the Veil, there's no protective cage, just the railing, and the open air, and the promise of a very long fall.

It worked before, I think, forcing myself toward the rail. Fear claws across my skin—fear of heights, fear of falling, fear that this will work, fear that it won't—but maybe fear is important. Fear goes with danger, with risk, the kind that draws poltergeists like moths to a flame.

I take a deep breath and get one foot up on the rail before Jacob grabs my arm and hauls me back to the ground, pale with fury. "What are you *doing*, Cass? Climbing onto a crypt is one thing. This is something else entirely. You're going to get yourself killed!"

"I'm not," I say, twisting free. "I just have to create the potential."

"I worked hard to save your life, and I'm not going to let you throw it away."

"I'm not throwing anything away, Jacob. I'm paying my debt. Doing my job."

"Why is *this* your job? Because Lara said so? She doesn't know *everything*. Even if she acts like she does. And I am not letting you get up on that rail."

"Fine," I snap. "I'll think of something else." I start pacing. "I just have to draw him out. There has to be a way to trap him, even just long enough for me to—"

"Enough!" shouts Jacob, all the humor gone from his voice. "Enough. Just admit why this is *really* so important to you."

I blink, confused. "What?"

"The second rule of friendship is no lies, Cass. Besides, it's literally *all* you've been thinking about since we got to Paris. So *admit* it. It's not just Thomas Laurent you're so worried about. It's *me*."

The words hit me like a punch.

"What? No, I'm—"

But then I hesitate.

I don't think I realized it.

But he's right.

It's not the only reason, but it's definitely one of them.

The truth is, I'm scared. Scared of Jacob's growing power, scared of what it means. Scared Lara was right. Scared of not being able to save my best friend.

"Scared I'm turning into some kind of *monster*?" Jacob growls, his eyes getting darker, his skin beginning to gray.

"Jacob—"

"Don't you trust me?"

"I do, but—"

"But you think I'm becoming the kind of ghost you're supposed to hunt. Well, the kind you *have* to. I mean, I'm already the kind you're *supposed* to, there's no forgetting that—"

"Stop!" I plead.

But Jacob is shaking with anger. "And just so you know," he says, "I still remember *everything*—everything—about my life, and the way it ended. I just don't want to share it with you."

"Why *not*?"

"Because it's none of your business!" he shouts, the hair rising up around his face, as if the air around him is turning to water. "Because I don't want to think about it!" His clothes begin to darken, as if wet. "And I don't want you to know because you won't look at me the same." His chest heaves, his shirt soaked through. "I won't be the boy who saved your life, I'll be the one who *died*, and—"

I throw my arms around his shoulders and hug him, as tightly as I can here in this place where I'm less solid and he's more real. And for a second, Jacob just stands there, and I don't know if he's still angry or just surprised. And then the fight goes out of him. His shoulders slump. His head tips forward against my shoulder.

"I don't know what's happening to me," he says. "I don't know what it means. It scares me, too. But I don't want to go. I don't want to lose you. Or myself."

I tighten my grip. "You're not going to," I say. "You have something the poltergeist doesn't."

"What's that?"

I pull back so he can see my face. "You have me."

He smiles, a thin imitation of his usual humor. But it's something.

I pull away, wiping my eyes quickly.

"*Viens,*" whispers a voice, and we both turn to see the ghost of a little old lady, hobbling toward us in a faded dress and coat, her skin worn deep with wrinkles. Her eyes are too bright, her smile wide and full of wooden teeth.

Jacob shakes his head, a nervous laugh escaping like steam as our world returns to normal.

How weird, that *this* is normal.

"*Viens avec moi,*" the old lady coos, one gnarled hand reaching forward.

Mom's story comes back to me. *The young woman's body was found on the stones below. The old lady was never seen again.*

"*Viens,*" the ghost urges, shuffling closer, and I'm very aware of the lack of railing behind me, the long fall.

"I've got your back," says Jacob, putting himself between me and the edge.

I draw out the pendant from my pocket, lifting the mirror to the old lady's eyes.

Her fingers close around my wrist.

"Viens avec . . ." she begins, trailing off as she catches her reflection.

This time, I remember the words right away.

"Watch and listen," I say.

Her eyes go flat and empty.

"See and know."

Her edges ripple.

"This is what you are."

The old woman's hand slips from my wrist. Her whole body goes thin, and I reach into the hollow of her chest and draw out the thread of her life, brittle and gray and lightless. It dissolves in my hand, blows away, and so does the old woman.

The bells are still ringing, but they sound far away, and the Veil begins to thin, losing its sharpness, its shape, without the ghost to hold it up.

Jacob rests a hand on my shoulder, and I turn back to him.

"Let's get out of here," I say, taking his hand.

The Veil parts, and we step through. I inhale deeply, trying to shake off the weirdness that always follows me back from the other side, and Jacob's hand goes thin in mine, dissolving back from flesh to something ever so slightly thicker than air.

There's a small squeak of surprise, and I realize Adele is staring at me, the place where I'm standing, the place where I obviously *wasn't* standing a second ago, her eyes wide and her mouth open in surprise.

CHAPTER TWENTY

T here you are," says Pauline, rounding the corner. "Let's go."

For once, Adele has nothing to say. All the way down the tower steps and out into the late-afternoon light, she simply stares at me, speechless.

By the time we reach the Rue de Rivoli, the stoplights are all flashing a warning yellow, and traffic has come to a standstill, horns blaring.

This is bad.

Very, very bad.

Beneath the awning of the Hotel Valeur, Anton hands the footage case to Dad so he and Mom can review the last pieces of film. Annette kisses Mom once on each cheek, and Pauline wishes us a pleasant night and starts to walk away, then stops herself, remembering.

"Cassidy, your film," she says. "Do you still want me to get it developed for you?"

I'd forgotten. I look down at my camera; there's only one photo left on the reel. I usher the whole TV crew—Mom and Dad, Pauline, Anton and Annette—together in the frame, Paris rising at their backs, and take the final shot. Then I crank the used film into its canister and thumb the latch on the back of the camera. It springs open, and I tip the small cylinder into my hand. I give it to Pauline, even as I wonder what will—and won't—show up on the film.

Pauline slips the cylinder into her pocket and promises to see us again before we leave tomorrow.

Tomorrow—it's hard to imagine, in part because Thomas is still rampaging across the city.

Tomorrow—which means I have less than a day to send him on.

I'm running out of time.

"Here's a crazy thought," says Jacob. "What if we just *leave*?"

I frown pointedly in his direction. *What?*

"Think about it," he presses. "Thomas might have been drawn to you in the beginning, but he's definitely moved on to bigger targets. Between that and your vile salt-and-sage pouches, I bet we could get out of Paris unscathed."

"And what would happen to *Paris*?" I mutter.

Anton and Annette wave goodbye, too. With the whole crew gone, we all turn to look at Adele, who shows absolutely no signs of leaving. She simply stares, as if *we're* the TV show and she wants to see what we'll do next.

"Should you be heading home?" asks Dad.

Adele rocks back and forth in her gold sneakers. "Do I have to?"

"Well, won't your mother be worried?"

Adele glances over her shoulder; the sun is just starting to sink, turning the edges of the sky orange. She shrugs. "Not yet."

"I have an idea!" says Mom, sliding her arm through Dad's. "Cass, your father and I are going to the salon for a drink. Why don't you two go up to the room and hang out. Introduce Adele to Grim." She hands me the show binder. "You can tell her all about *The Inspecters*."

Dad passes me the footage case and asks me to take it upstairs, and my parents stroll off across the lobby.

Back in the hotel suite, I set the footage case aside,

and Adele lets out a delighted squeak and scoops up a very stunned Grim, speaking softly to him in French. Meanwhile, I take out the photographs she brought me and spread them on the floor, hoping they will help me think.

Soon my cell rings. A video call.

It's Lara. She's doesn't bother with small talk. "Have you seen the news?"

"Hold on." I find the remote and click the TV on. A news anchor talks briskly, a video playing above her shoulder. On that smaller screen, emergency lights flare atop a car.

It's all in French, of course, but the message is painfully clear.

"Oh."

On the TV, the news anchor cuts away to a woman sitting on the sidewalk while a medic presses a cloth to the side of her head. In the background, a multi-car collision clogs an intersection. I change the channel and see a map of the Metro covered in red outage markers.

I mute the TV, and Lara sits forward in her chair. "I warned you this would happen. Poltergeists are—" She stops abruptly, frowns. "Cassidy," she says tightly, "who is that?"

I glance over my shoulder and see Adele perched on the arm of the sofa, Grim a mound of fur on her lap. "Oh yeah. That's Adele."

Adele tugs the lollipop out of her mouth and waves cheerfully. "Hello!"

Lara does not wave back.

"Are you a ghost hunter, too?" asks Adele.

At that, Lara goes very still, her dark eyes furious. "Cassidy Blake," she hisses through clenched teeth. "What have you *told* her?"

"Not much," I answer, at the same time Adele says, "Everything!"

Lara's expression shifts from anger to horror. "Why would you do that?"

"I have to say," muses Jacob, "it's so nice to see that anger directed at someone else."

"Be quiet, ghost," she growls. "Cassidy, explain."

"It just kind of came up," I say.

"Oh yes, because spectral abilities are such a natural topic of conversation."

"Look," I explain. "I went to see Richard Laurent's granddaughter, Sylvaine, but she wouldn't talk to me.

Adele's her daughter. She tracked me down and brought me photographs—"

"Wait," cuts in Lara. "What photographs?"

I turn the phone so she can see the pictures spread on the floor.

"Closer," says Lara, and I crouch, panning the phone over them. Adele drops down cross-legged beside them. She reaches for a picture with only Thomas, looking back over his shoulder and flashing a wide smile.

"And you're still no closer?" asks Lara. "To finding out what—"

"Such a sad story," murmurs Adele, "what happened to Thomas."

The room goes quiet. Jacob and I both stare. Even Lara's mouth is hanging open on the screen.

"*You know?*" we all say at once.

Adele shifts a little. "*Oui,*" she says. "Maman told me. She doesn't like to talk about the past, not with strangers, but she said it is important to know one's history. She said it is private. But if it will help you help Thomas," she adds, "I will tell you the story."

CHAPTER TWENTY-ONE

It is a very sad story," begins Adele, drawing Grim into her lap.

"My great-grandfather Richard was ten when it happened. He was three years older than Thomas, and he was Thomas's hero. They were close. Like this—" She crosses her fingers. "Thomas used to follow Richard around. And Richard let him. All summer," she continues, "Richard and a few other boys had been sneaking down into the Catacombs at night."

"How?" asks Lara.

Adele shrugs. "Now there is only one entrance and one exit, but there used to be more. If you knew how to look for them. Richard did." Adele flashes a small, mischievous smile. "So they would sneak down in the dark."

Jacob and I both shudder a little at the thought of the Catacombs at night. The tunnel of bones lit only by candles or flashlights, some pale illumination that leaves the skeletons buried in shadow.

"And Thomas wanted to go, too. He begged and begged until one night, Richard finally agreed to take him."

I glance at Jacob as Adele talks. His face is clouded, all the expression gone, as if his mind has wandered off while listening. But he must feel me looking because he blinks and cuts his gaze toward me, one eyebrow raised.

"And so they went," continues Adele, stroking Grim. "Thomas, Richard, and two of Richard's friends. Down into the dark."

The cat is a puddle of black fur in her lap, the happiest I've seen him since getting to Paris. Adele must have a gift for befriending cranky cats.

"The boys were always playing games, and so that is what they did. They played *cache-cache*. Do you know what that is?"

I shake my head.

"You call it hide-and-seek."

I jerk upright. "The counting!" I say, and Lara nods on the screen.

"*Quoi?*" asks Adele, looking between us. "What?"

"*Un, deux, trois, quatre, cinq . . .*" recites Lara in her flawless French. "I couldn't understand why he'd be going *up* instead of *down*."

"But if they were playing hide-and-seek," I say, "and he was the seeker . . ."

Adele nods eagerly. "Thomas was too small, too good at hiding," she says, "so they made him search instead. He closed his eyes to count, and the other boys all ran and hid."

I imagine playing such a game down there, hiding, pressed against skeletons or climbing over bones, and I shudder.

"Thomas was very good at finding the other boys, no matter where they hid," Adele goes on. "So on the third game, Richard agreed to let his little brother hide."

My stomach twists as I realize where this is going.

"Richard was the seeker," says Adele, "and he found one of his friends, and then the other, but no Thomas. Richard searched for almost an hour, before he finally gave up. The boys were tired. They wanted to go home. So Richard called out, 'Thomas, *c'est finit*'—'it's over'—but there was no answer, except for his own voice, echoing in the tunnels."

A shiver runs through me. If it were any other story, I might delight in the nervous thrill. But I have *seen* this small boy in his dirt-scuffed clothes. And I can picture him lost down there, hidden among the bones or wandering the tunnels, turned around, alone.

Adele goes on. "Richard stayed down there all night, searching for his brother. But he couldn't find him. Finally, he had no choice. He went home and told his parents, who called the police, and they organized a search."

I swallow hard. "Did they find Thomas? Eventually?"

Adele nods. "They did," she says slowly. "But by then it was too late. He was already . . ." She trails off.

My chest tightens around the next question. "Where did they find him?"

Adele hesitates, petting Grim. "He was very good at hiding. He had climbed into one of the little . . ." She hesitates, searching for the word, then makes an arch with her hand. *"Coin."*

"Nook," translates Lara. "Like an alcove."

Adele nods. *"Oui.* That. Anyway, he climbed in, nice and small. But the bones around him were old, and sometimes . . ." She makes a small, collapsing motion with her hands. "They slip. Sections fall."

On the phone, Lara puts a hand to her mouth.

"They found him, in the end, beneath the bones."

Jacob shivers a little, and I tense at the thought of being buried down there in the dark.

"And Richard?" I ask.

Adele leans forward over Grim—he doesn't seem to mind—and taps a photo of the older boy, standing alone. There's a sliver of empty space beside him, his arm faintly outstretched, as if Richard doesn't know where to rest his elbow without his little brother's shoulder.

"My mother said he was always sad. He never forgave himself for losing his brother down there."

We sit in silence for several long moments. The only sound is the steady rumble of Grim's purring.

And as I turn the story over in my head, I realize, with grim dread, exactly what I have to do.

"Don't say it, Cass," interjects Jacob.

"We have to go back to the Catacombs."

Adele looks up from the cat, her face going white. "What?"

Jacob groans.

"Think about it," I press. "Just because Thomas isn't *bound* to one place, that doesn't mean that place isn't important to him. The Catacombs are where he *died*."

"Sure," counters Jacob, "but he *doesn't remember dying there*."

"Maybe not consciously," I say, "but when he saw us, he was *counting*."

"So?"

"So some part of him remembers playing hide-and-seek down there," says Lara from my phone, "even if he doesn't *remember* remembering. His memory of the Catacombs would probably have been one of the last things to go. Which means it will be the first to come back. It makes sense. It will be the easiest place to remind him."

I turn to the phone again. "Okay, Lara," I say. "I'll take it from here."

"Good luck," she says, right before I hang up.

"Does it *have* to be the Catacombs?" Jacob asks me. "Why can't we pick a level playing field? Like a garden. A garden seems nice. And *aboveground*."

I wish we could do that. I really do. But I've wasted too much time trying to lure Thomas out, make him come to me, avoiding the simple truth: The Catacombs are where it started. It's where it has to end.

"You know I'm right about this."

"No, I don't," says Jacob. "There's, like, a fifty percent chance you're right, and a ninety percent chance this is going to go really wrong."

I smirk. "Only ninety?" I ask.

"What is your ghost saying?" asks Adele, rising to her feet, the cat clutched against her front like a shield.

Jacob crosses his arms, ignoring Adele. "What if Thomas doesn't show up?" he asks me.

But he will.

I can feel it.

The way I feel the tapping when ghosts are near.

The way I feel the Veil against my fingers.

"Fine," says Jacob, "but how are we supposed to get back into the Catacombs? Last time I checked, your parents are done filming, the place is probably closed, and we're leaving tomorrow."

My heart sinks.

It's not that I don't have an idea.

I have one, and it's really, really bad.

Jacob grimaces as he reads my mind. "Oh *no*."

CHAPTER TWENTY-TWO

The footage is stored in the dark metal briefcase.

I crouch in front of it, hands resting on the clasps.

"Adele," I say, "I need you to go into the hall and keep an eye out."

She frowns. "How do you *keep an eye*?"

"It's an expression," I say. "It means I need to you to keep watch. Tell me when the coast is clear."

"The coast? As in the sea?"

I fumble for words, exasperated. "Just go stand in the hall, and knock on the door if you see my parents coming."

She sets Grim down and goes outside, and I take a deep breath and release the clasps.

"Wait," says Jacob. "Look, you know I'm always up for a bit of bad behavior—"

"No, you're not," I say. "You are a total wuss."

"Okay, no need for names. Just listen. There's bad, and then there's *bad*. And what you're about to do is *bad*."

"I *know*," I hiss. "But there's also ghosts, and then there's *poltergeists*. And what we're dealing with," I say, gesturing at the muted TV, "is a poltergeist."

On the screen, emergency vehicles surround a building that definitely looks like it's on fire. A second later, the shot cuts away to a busy street, all the traffic stopped as maintenance crews try to get near a sparking power line.

Jacob sighs, defeated, as I ease the lid up.

The case is divided in two. Compact film reels are set into the black foam on one side, and digital cards are slotted on the other. Of course. The crew films both ways. Lucky for me, everything is carefully labeled, broken down not only by day but by location.

The first reel has been labeled CAT. Short for Catacombs.

I brush my fingertips across the label. The Catacombs are one of the most famous sites in the world. No ghost trip to Paris is complete without it. So if I destroy the footage from that session, then we'll *have* to go back.

Jacob clears his throat. "You know, I thought you

climbing into an open grave and hiding beneath a corpse was a bad idea, Cass, but this is making that look positively sensible."

"I have to do this, Jacob."

"No, you *don't*." He crouches beside me. "This isn't like what happened in Scotland. You're not trapped in the Veil. You have a choice here. And when you think about it, this poltergeist isn't really our problem."

"He *is*, though. And even if he weren't, we're the only ones who can send him on, Jacob. If we don't do something, people could get hurt."

"*We* could get hurt!" says Jacob. I give him a measuring look. "Well, *you* could," he amends. "Which is bad enough."

I rock back on my heels. "Spider-Man's Law."

"What?"

"You know what I'm talking about. With great power . . ." I trail off, waiting for him to finish the line.

Jacob mumbles in reply. ". . . mums ray resons . . ."

"What was that?" I press.

He scuffs his shoe along the floor. ". . . comes great responsibility."

"Exactly."

Jacob shifts, sighs. "I can't believe you Spider-Man'ed me," he grumbles as I reach for the film.

Jacob covers his eyes, as if he can't look.

Unfortunately, I have to.

I solemnly swear that I am up to no good, I think as I pluck Catacombs data card from its slot in the foam and slip it into my back pocket.

"Some days I really wish you were Slythercore instead of Gryffindot," mutters Jacob.

"No, you don't," I say, freeing the reel of film marked CAT. "And one of these days I'm going to make you *read* Harry Potter." I turn the plastic case over in my hands.

"How exactly are you going to explain the sudden destruction?" asks Jacob. "Are you going to blame the poltergeist? Think your parents will believe that?"

I look at the label again, considering.

CAT.

Nearby, Grim stretches and yawns.

"No," I say, pulling the tape from the reels. "But cats are fond of ribbons, aren't they?"

*   *   *

Five minutes later, the stage is set, the damage is done. Adele comes in and says she can hear my parents on the stairs. I grab her by the arm and race out into the hall, determined to meet them on the way.

"Oh, there you are," I say as we run into them on the stairs. "We were just coming to find you."

"Everything okay?" asks Mom.

"Yeah," I say, a little too fast. "We were just getting hungry and wanted to know if we could order food."

"Sure," says Mom as we turn around and start back up.

I hold my breath as we climb the stairs.

The last part of my plan rests on Jacob, or rather, on his growing powers.

"You're sure you're strong enough to do it?" I asked, balancing the case on the edge of the table.

"I think so," he said. He reached out, eyes narrowed in concentration, and pressed one finger to the corner of the case. It tipped, ever so slightly, before regaining its balance.

Now, as we reach the hall, I sneeze once loudly, the agreed-upon signal, and a second later—

CRASH.

The sound of a metal film case toppling.

Mom bursts into the room, Dad right behind her. Adele and I linger in the hallway, but judging by Mom's gasp of horror and Dad's cursing, it worked.

The scene stretches before us, a picture of destruction.

Grim, jolted upright by the sound of the case, stares down at the mess on the floor in front of him. Only a few of the digital cards fell out of the case. The rest stayed lodged in their foam slots. The film reels weren't so lucky. They roll away, tip over, most of them unharmed, but one lies ruined in the center of the scene, a mess of knotted film.

"Bad cat!" shouts Mom, rushing forward.

Grim leaps up onto the back of the sofa and glowers at me with his green eyes as if to say, *Low blow, human.* I silently vow to buy him a whole tin of catnip when this is over.

"Mon dieu!" says Adele. I have to hand it to her, her face is a picture of surprise, whereas I just feel like throwing up.

Jacob perches on the back of the couch, arms crossed, clearly torn between feeling annoyed at me and smug about his accomplishment. He settles for watching as the four of us search on our hands and knees, recovering all the spilled reels and the fallen data cards, fitting them back into the briefcase.

Dad tries to feed the ruined film back into the plastic shell, but it quickly becomes obvious it's not going to work.

"Good thing there's a digital backup," he grumbles, but Mom only shakes her head.

"It's missing."

"*What?*" demands Dad, looking inside the case to confirm what I already know.

They won't find the Catacombs data chip there. Or anywhere.

Dad's face is red with anger, Mom's pale and blotchy with distress, and there's a storm inside my stomach as I remind myself that people's lives are in danger. That I have to do the right thing, even if the right thing in this instance has a dose of wrong mixed in.

Still, it doesn't feel good.

And I must look as bad as I feel, because Jacob doesn't give me a hard time. Instead, he appears at my side and rests his shoulder against the air right next to mine.

"Spider-Man's Law," he says as tears threaten to spill down my cheeks.

I nod, silently promising that if this doesn't work, I will find a way to make it up to them.

All of them.

Including the cat.

"Hey," I say, as if the idea has just occurred to me. "We don't leave until tomorrow afternoon, right? So why don't we just go back and film it again in the morning?"

"It's not that simple, Cassidy," says Dad, pinching the bridge of his nose.

My heart trips over its beat. "Why not?"

Dad sighs. "The Catacombs are a public site. Admission is tightly controlled. We can't simply come and go as we please. Pauline arranged our visit weeks in advance."

I look to Mom, but she's already a step ahead, her cell phone pressed to her ear. I can only assume she's talking to Pauline.

"I know," Mom is saying over and over, leaving us with only patches of silence to wonder what Pauline is saying. "Is there any way? All right."

She lets the cell slip from her ear with a shuddering sigh.

"Well?" asks Dad.

"She's going to see what she can do."

So we do the only thing we can.

We wait.

Five agonizing minutes later, the cell rings, and I hold my breath as Mom answers. I watch her face, the tension finally replaced by a flood of relief. I feel it like fresh air in my lungs as Mom says, "Thank you. Thank you so much." She hangs up, explains that Pauline, blessed, wonderful Pauline, has arranged for us to go into the Catacombs after hours.

Tonight.

"That's great!" I say.

"Yeah, great," echoes Jacob. "Because the only thing scarier than being a hundred feet underground during the day is being there at night."

And even though Adele can't hear what he said, she looks similarly unsettled by the idea of a trip to the tombs in the dark.

My parents get dressed again in their on-screen wear, smooth their hair, and try to recover a semblance of calm as they wait for Pauline to arrive. But when Dad sees me pulling on my shoes, he shakes his head.

"No, Cass. You and Adele stay here."

My stomach drops. "If you're going back, I want to come."

"There's no reason," says Mom. "It scared you enough the first time, and—"

"I won't get in the way," I promise. "Please."

"It's not about you getting in the *way*, honey," says Mom.

"But you couldn't wait to get out of there last time," cuts in Dad. "Why the change of heart?"

Well, I think, *there's this poltergeist I need to lure out so I can remind him who he is and how he died, then send him on before anyone else gets hurt.*

But I can't exactly say that, so I take a different tactic.

"The Catacombs are the kind of place most people only see once," I say. "I don't want to lose the chance to see them again. Even if they're kind of scary. Besides, you gave me a job, to take photos. I want to do it."

I can see them bending, but I throw in one last angle. "Plus, I want to show Adele."

Adele looks at me with something less than enthusiasm, but I silently will her not to say anything.

Mom sighs, but Dad only shakes his head and checks his

watch. "If you're coming, you should put on a jacket. It's colder at night."

I resist the urge to throw my arms around his waist. There's happy, and then there's suspiciously excited, and I can't afford for them to wonder.

Luckily, they have plenty on their minds.

Pauline meets us in the lobby.

She's opted for a hired car. Anton and Annette are already seated inside. Dad hands off the film to them with a round of profuse apology, but Anton waves him off and takes the case.

"C'est la vie," he says. "Things happen."

"Unless you're Cassidy Blake," says Jacob as the car pulls away. "And then you *make* them happen."

CHAPTER TWENTY-THREE

It's dark by the time we pull up in front of the little green shack.

A security officer is waiting as we climb out onto the curb, and I snap a photo of the entrance sign with my phone and send it to Lara.

> Me:
> Going in. Hope to make things right.

> Me:
> If I die, don't reap Jacob.

I switch the phone off, slip it into my pocket, and take a deep breath.

Confession: I'm pretty scared. Scared that my plan will work. Scared that it won't. Scared of what's waiting down there in the dark.

I wish the sun were still up.

I know it shouldn't make a difference—after all, it's

always dark down there, beneath the earth. It *shouldn't* make a difference, but it does. As we walk toward the door, I can feel that shift Mom always talks about, in the way the world tastes and feels when the sun goes down.

No warmth in the air to keep the chill at bay.

No light to push the shadows back.

I *know* the dark is no more haunted than the day.

Or rather, the day is no less haunted than the dark. But it's still a whole lot scarier.

"Ghost five, for luck," says Jacob, holding his palm low instead of high. I bring my hand to rest just above it.

For luck, I think, but instead of making the usual sound of skin hitting skin, we both leave the gesture quiet. We let our hands linger, one above the other. The closest we can get to comfort.

My hand drifts up to the camera around my neck. I didn't actually load a new film cartridge, but it's still a talisman. A good-luck charm. A little extra bit of magic. And of course, its bright white flash is always good for stopping ghosts.

The security officer slips a heavy key into the lock and slides back the iron gate, just far enough for us to squeeze through. I think of Thomas, so small he could simply slide between the last bar and the wall.

The crew goes through first, then Mom, then Dad. I'm about to follow when I realize Adele isn't with me. I look back and see her hovering on the threshold, her gold sneakers shifting nervously on the curb. She's biting her lip, looking past me into the darkened hut.

"Alors," she says softly. "You know, it's getting late." She keeps her chin lifted, her head high. "I should probably go home."

Up until now, she's been so bold, so brave, it was easy to forget: She's still a kid.

"You're right," I said. "Your mom is probably getting worried."

"Yes," she says. "It's not that I don't want to go," she adds with a proud sniff. "It's just . . ."

"It's okay," I say, putting my hand on her shoulder. "You've been so helpful. I couldn't have gotten this far without you. But I'll take it from here."

Her sharp eyes find mine. "You're sure you can do it?"

No, I think. I'm a mile from sure. But what I say is, "I hope so."

Adele swallows and nods. "Okay."

My hand falls away from her shoulder. She's starting to walk away when I have an idea.

"Wait," I call, ducking back inside the green hut. I run up to Dad and tug the salt-and-sage pouch from the inside pocket of his coat. He'll have to do with one less charm.

"Where did that come from?" he asks, but I'm already heading back toward Adele.

Jacob shuffles away, holding his breath, as I give her the little pouch. "To keep you safe," I say. Adele looks down at the pouch, and then throws her arms around my waist.

"*Bonne chance*, Cassidy Blake."

"Is that French for *be careful*?"

Adele shakes her head.

"No," she says with a smile. "It means *good luck*."

I smile back. "*Merci*, Adele Laurent."

"Bye, pipsqueak," adds Jacob as the girl heads for the Metro station down the block.

"Cassidy!" calls Mom from inside the hut, and I take a deep breath.

"You ready for this?" asks Jacob.

"Not really."

He swallows. "But we're going to do it anyway, aren't we?"

I square my shoulders toward the door. "Yeah. We are."

We follow the rest of the group through the turnstile, pausing at the top of the spiral steps that coil tightly down into the dark. Mom and Dad go first, followed by Anton and Annette, their cameras up on their shoulders, the red lights a signal that they're already rolling. Then me, Jacob, and Pauline.

Six sets of steps echoing on the stairs.

Un, deux, trois, I count as we head down one floor, two, three. *Quatre, cinq,* I finish as we reach the bottom.

A breeze, stale and cold, wafts toward us, as if the tunnels are breathing.

I pull my jacket close, the old photographs of Thomas and his family rustling faintly beneath it. And then we start the ten-minute walk through the empty tunnels toward the entrance of the Empire of the Dead.

Water drips from the low ceiling. Footsteps echo off damp stone.

"Now?" asks Jacob. He shoves his hands in his pockets, clearly eager to get this over with.

I shake my head. Thomas and Richard wouldn't have played their games out here, where there are no twists and turns, nothing to hide behind. No, they'd have been farther in, where the halls begin to wind and the walls are full of bones and shadows.

But I can't blame Jacob for wanting this to be over.

The air is damp and cold, and every step we take is one step away from safety. The Veil begins to get heavier. It leans against me, pushing me forward, trying to drag me across the line, into the dark.

Not yet, I think, pushing back. *Not yet*.

We reach the end of the galleries.

ARRÉTE! warns the sign over the doorway. STOP!

We've come too far to turn back now.

And so, with a deep breath, we step through.

PART FIVE

MEMORY

CHAPTER TWENTY-FOUR

Buried beneath Paris, the Catacombs are home to more than six million bones . . ."

My parents walk ahead, recounting the history and the lore of this place. They're telling the same stories as before, but the energy is different this time. They are clearly on edge, ruffled from the whole briefcase incident. It makes them tense and jumpy in a way that's probably great for a show about paranormal activity. Even Dad's usual unflappable calm has tightened, making him seem, for once, truly nervous.

Mom's voice is tense, even as her hand dances through the air over the skulls.

"The tunnels snake beneath the city, so vast that most Parisians are walking on bones . . ."

"Now?" asks Jacob, and I nod, knowing this is the closest I'll get to a chance. I back away one step, two, and then turn, about to reach for the Veil when a hand catches my wrist.

Pauline.

"Don't go wandering," she warns, careful to keep her voice low, because everything echoes here.

"I'm not," I whisper, lifting the camera a little. "I was just looking for a good shot." I point over her shoulder toward my parents, who are still walking away. The glow of the tunnel lights ahead of them creates an eerie halo, turning them to silhouettes.

Pauline's grip loosens, and I see my chance.

By the time her hand falls away, I'm already reaching for the Veil. It parts around me, and the last thing I see is Pauline turning back, her eyes widening in surprise as I vanish through the invisible curtain.

My heart lurches with panic as I'm plunged back into the dark.

The air is heavy and stale. All I can think is that I'm five stories underground and last time there was a lantern on the ground, but now there's not, and I can't breathe. Panic fills the place where air should be, and it takes all my strength not to reach for the Veil and cross back into the safety of the light.

"Jacob," I whisper, half-afraid that no one will answer. Half-afraid that someone else will. But then I feel him, a shift in the air beside me.

"Cass," he whispers back, and I realize that I can almost, almost see the outline of his face. I blink, desperate for my eyes to adjust, and when they do, I realize that the darkness isn't absolute.

There must be a light somewhere, around the corner, the thinnest glow spilling through the tunnels. I make my way forward, keeping one hand against the wall for balance. The wall that isn't a wall of course, but a stack of bones. My fingers skip over the hollows of a skull, the dips and grooves where bones lock together like puzzle pieces.

We round the corner, and I find the oil lamp on the ground. I crouch and turn the knob up, and the tunnel brightens a little, but not nearly as much as I'd like. I look around, but there's no sign of Thomas. No sign of anyone, for that matter. The tunnels are empty.

"Thomas?" I call. But all I hear is my own voice echoing back. And there's no sign of him, or the red light that seems to trail him through the Veil.

But he has to be here. He has to.

And if he's not?

I look down at the lantern on the dirt floor, then straighten. I have an idea.

"Hey, Jacob," I say. "Want to play a game of hide-and-seek?"

He looks at me for a long moment, then swallows and holds out his hands. One fist rests in the other open palm: the universal gesture for rock-paper-scissors.

"Winner hides," he says. "Loser seeks."

"No way," I say. Rock-paper-scissors isn't a fair game when one of us is psychic. I pull a coin from my back pocket and flip it.

"Tails," calls Jacob as the coin glints in the dark.

I catch the coin, slap it against the back of my hand.

Heads.

I'm relieved. The only thing creepier than being down here in the dark would be closing my eyes. Jacob groans and turns to face the nearest column of bones, putting his hands over his eyes.

"One, two, three . . ." he begins.

And instead of running to hide, I slip into a shadowed

gap nearby, and wait. Wait for movement. Wait for the sight of red eyes in a small round face. I chew my lip.

Jacob gets to ten, and there's still no sign of Thomas.

Fifteen.

Twenty.

And then, just as Jacob is saying "Twenty-one," I hear the shuffle of feet. I look up and see Thomas. The little boy peers around the corner, red eyes wide with curiosity. He doesn't see me. But he sees Jacob. He watches Jacob for a long moment, then turns and slips away into the dark.

I follow, careful to keep just enough distance that he doesn't know I'm there, but not so much that I lose him. It helps that his whole body is tinged with red. His edges glow, the air around him curling with wisps of colored smoke. I slip along in his wake, and soon he stops and crouches. He folds himself into a low arch, the bones beneath long crumbled.

Just like the nook in Adele's story.

I squat in front of Thomas's hiding place.

"Caught you," I whisper. But for a moment, all I see is darkness, shadow, and I think he somehow got away. And then I realize he's there. His head was down, bowed against his folded arms. Now he looks up, red eyes glowing in the dark.

And *scowls*.

I jerk backward, shocked by the anger in that small face. The venom in his look as he crawls out from his hiding place, red eyes so bright they seem to burn the air in front of him.

"Thomas . . ." I start, drawing the photos from my jacket as he gets to his feet.

His expression flashes with the kind of temper that only a kid his age can muster. Indignation. Betrayal.

He mutters something in French, and even though I don't understand the words, the sentiment is clear. I cheated. I didn't play fair.

"Thomas," I say again, trying to keep my voice steady. I hold out one of the photos of him and his brother, but he doesn't even look. His eyes slide past the images, like oil on water, and land on me.

And then his hand shoots out with lightning speed.

I jump back, assuming he's aiming for me. But instead, he slams his hand against the nearest wall of bones like a child knocking over blocks.

Only these blocks don't fall.

They tremble and shake, glowing red with the force of his power.

Outside the Veil, Thomas was strong.

Here, inside it, fueled by all that mischief and menace and mayhem, he's something else entirely. As if he can pull on the energy of the space itself, on the restless dead, on the centuries of loss and fear and sadness. The Catacombs bend around him, to him. This isn't just a tomb for him.

It's a playground.

And as the walls shake, something begins to seep through them, leaking between the bones like smoke. And then it takes form. A young couple with backpacks. A teenage girl with lank black hair. A middle-aged man with a disheveled beard. They come one, two, five, ten, and as the spirits pour out of the bone-strewn walls, shuffling, grimacing, angry, I retreat, realizing with horror that the Catacombs have never been that empty.

They were just asleep.

My camera flies up, my index finger already hitting the flash. The bright glare buys me a second.

And in that second, I turn and run.

CHAPTER TWENTY-FIVE

My shoes slip on the damp stone.

I hit the end of the tunnel before a ragged old man rises up through the floor, blocking my way. I skid backward on my heels and tear down another, darker path, dragging the necklace over my head right before I collide with another body. I'm already bringing the mirror up when a familiar hand catches my wrist.

"Jacob," I gasp, turning the mirror away from him.

He looks over my shoulder, his eyes widening at the tide of spirits, the rumbling bones.

"What did you *do*?" he demands.

"I found Thomas," I say, pulling Jacob after me. A gate hangs open up ahead, and we stumble through. I turn and slam the iron bars shut behind us.

"Upside," I say, breathless, "Thomas is definitely here now. Downside," I add, sinking back against the bars, "he's stronger than I expected."

I close my eyes as a wave of dizziness washes over me, the Veil beginning to steal my strength, my focus.

"So what's the plan?" asks Jacob, and I'm about to reply when he pulls me away from the gate, seconds before a hand shoots through.

A woman stands beyond the bars, reaching for me, whispering a stream of desperate French. I hold the mirror out, trapping her attention.

"Watch and listen. See and know. This is what you are."

Her eyes widen a fraction, and I thrust my hand into her chest, pulling out her thread. She crumbles, but before she's even gone, the walls are shaking, rousing more spirits, and I know the only way to stop them all is to stop the one who woke them up.

Thomas.

I back away from the bars.

"Come on," I say, grabbing Jacob's hand. We can't stay here.

"We can't just keep running, either," says Jacob.

"I know," I say. "I'm just buying time to—"

We round another corner, and a spirit—a middle-aged man in old-fashioned clothes—slides forward out of the dark.

"*Chérie, chérie,*" he sings, and I don't know who Chérie is, but something about the ghost catches my eye. Not the concerning lack of teeth in his grin.

It's his hat.

A newsboy cap, the kind with a stiff front brim.

I've seen one just like it, in the old photos I have in my pocket. And suddenly, I have an idea.

Jacob is already backing away from the specter, but I rush forward.

"Excuse me," I say, "could I borrow your—"

The man snarls and grabs me, shoving me against a wall of bones that rattle as they dig into my back. I gasp, but I manage to swipe the cap from his head before Jacob lunges at the spirit from behind, hauling him backward.

Freed, I slump against the bones, and Jacob slams the other ghost into a pillar of skulls. The bones topple with a crash, and the man drops, dazed, to his hands and knees.

"Come on!" says Jacob, but my gaze flicks from Jacob's shirt, with its large comic book emblem, to the man's jacket, weathered and old. I press the stolen cap into Jacob's hands and reach for the fallen ghost, plucking at one of his gray cuffs.

"A little help?" I snap at Jacob when he just stands there, looking from the cap in his hands to me.

"Help you do *what*?" he demands.

"Get—this—coat—" I say, tugging at the ghost's sleeve. The spirit is beginning to fight back, but with Jacob's help, I manage to wrestle the jacket off the dim-witted spirit, a task just as difficult and awkward as it sounds.

I toss the coat to Jacob and shove the mirror into the spirit's face, reaping his thread as quickly as possible. By the time he vanishes, I'm already doubling back down the tunnel, searching for the right place to set my trap.

"Are you going to tell me what is going on?" asks Jacob, clutching the coat and hat as he follows me.

Finally, I find it.

A stretch of tunnel lit by an oil lamp, one side dissolving into darkness, and the other capped by a dead end.

I turn toward Jacob. "Time for a different kind of game. Put those on."

He looks at me, aghast. "You want me to play dress-up in another ghost's clothes?"

I pull out one of the photos. The shot of Richard, standing alone after Thomas's death. "I want you to dress up as *him*."

Jacob looks at the photograph for a long moment, and I wait for his witty retort, but he says nothing, only stares, his face unreadable.

"What?" I say. "You don't think it will work?"

But when he answers, his voice is low, strangely sober.

"Actually," he says, "I think it might."

He shrugs on the coat, grimacing a little.

"I feel so gross right now," he mumbles. The coat is big on him, big enough to cover the T-shirt, probably too big to look natural, but it's all we have to work with. He rolls up the sleeves.

"Sorry," I say.

"Well?" he says, adjusting the cap on his head. "How do I look?"

I look him up and down, surprised by the difference a few small changes make. In the coat and hat, Jacob could almost pass for an old-fashioned boy.

I glance from the photo of Richard to Jacob.

"One more thing," I say. Then I drag my hand along the top of a low stack of bones and wipe the dirt along his cheeks.

Jacob grits his teeth. "Did you seriously just wipe dead-people dirt on me?"

The resemblance isn't perfect, of course.

But it might just be enough.

It better be, because I'm running out of options.

And out of time.

My vision is beginning to swim a little, and I know I've been down here too long.

"You owe me so many comics," Jacob says, but the joke is thin, and I can tell he's unsettled. Even scared. I forget, sometimes, that so much of Jacob's fear is an act, made to make me feel braver.

Seeing him genuinely afraid is, well, terrifying.

I tell Jacob the rest of my plan, then point to the nearest tower of bones.

The skulls form a wavy band every two feet, grinning out at us with empty eyes. I use them as a handhold, and Jacob laces his fingers and gives me a leg up, helping me hoist myself onto the top of the wall. That's how I think of it. A wall. Not a stack of femurs and skulls, the bones shifting dangerously under my weight. Nope. Just a wall. A place to crouch, to hide, to wait. The ceiling overhead is low and damp, and I cringe as it brushes the top of my head, try not to think too hard about any of it.

From this angle, Jacob's face is hidden by his borrowed cap, and it's not hard to imagine he's someone else. A boy looking for his little brother.

"Thomas!" he calls out, voice ringing through the tunnels.

Thomas . . . Thomas . . .

For a long moment, nothing happens.

"Thomas?"

. . . Thomas . . . Thomas . . .

And then.

The little boy comes out of nowhere. He doesn't peer around a corner, doesn't come running. One second, Jacob is alone in the tunnel. The next, he's not.

Jacob doesn't see him, not at first.

He's got his back to the boy as he calls into the dark.

"Thomas!"

. . . Thomas . . . Thomas . . .

The boy tilts his head, confused, and the red light in his eyes flickers once, like a shorting bulb, but then comes back. He takes a step forward, then stops when his foot comes down on the slip of paper. One of the photographs I've scattered through this stretch of tunnel like bread crumbs, meant to lead a lost boy home.

I watch as Thomas crouches and picks up the photo. He stares at the shot of Richard with his hand on his little brother's shoulder. His eyes narrow. The red light flickers again.

It's *working*.

Jacob keeps walking, just like we agreed, and Thomas follows.

The bones beneath me dig into my palms as I creep forward.

Thomas kneels, picking up another photograph. And another. And another. The red light around him weakens with each slip of paper. Each memory.

I keep crawling, trying to keep pace as he makes his way toward Jacob.

The front layer of the wall is rigid beneath me, the bones locked to form a rough but stable structure. But the piles *behind* that facade are nothing but stacks of rotting old bones, so I'm careful to stay on the narrow strip of solid ground.

Up ahead, the tunnel ends.

Jacob stops, lifts one hand to the bones that bar his way, and then turns back.

I can't see his face, but his whole body stiffens in surprise at the sight of the boy clutching those old photos. Either he's a better actor than I thought, or he genuinely didn't hear Thomas coming up behind him.

"Thomas," he says, and I can hear him fighting to keep his voice steady.

Hold on, I think as the air coils nervously around Thomas.

"Richard?"

Thomas's voice is quiet, uncertain.

Jacob holds out his hand, and Thomas is about to reach for it. The red light in his eyes is almost gone, and I'm almost there when my knee comes down on a brittle bone—

And the bone snaps. Not enough for me to slip, but the sound rings out through the dark like a branch breaking in a silent forest.

Thomas twists away from Jacob, the red light surging back into his eyes. I cut sideways, out of his sight, and into the deeper dark.

Too late, I realize my mistake.

Too late, all my weight shifts from the stable wall to the stack of rotting bones.

Too late, and the pile gives way, crumbling like ash beneath me, and I'm falling down, down, down into the dark.

CHAPTER TWENTY-SIX

There are many kinds of dark.

There's the warm, reddish dark you see when you close your eyes.

There's the rich dark of a movie theater, the audience lit only by the screen.

And then there's the true dark of lightless spaces underground, places where the black is so thick you can't see your own hands. Can't see the lines of your body. Can't see any of the things you know are there with you in the dark.

This is that kind of dark.

I cough, my lungs filling with ash and soot. Something digs into my side. And for a moment, all I can think is, *This is how he died*. Thomas, buried by bones.

But I'm still alive.

I'm still alive.

Even if I can't see.

And then I remember my phone. I scramble to pull it out—there's no service down here, but I don't need to make a call. I just need some light. I turn the phone on and activate its built-in flashlight. The world around me bursts into glaring white light. The sight is . . . unpleasant. I'm on my back at the bottom of the hole, the edges above me flaking with dust. I get to my hands and knees, trying to hold my breath against the plume of death and decay as I swing the phone's light. The hole isn't deep, maybe four feet. I can reach up, curl my fingers back over the edge, but the crumbling bones are soft in places, sharp in others. And every time I move, the air fills with things I don't want to breathe, don't want to think about.

"Cassidy!" calls Jacob, his voice tight with panic.

"I'm all right!" I call back.

"Well, I'm not!"

I look around, nothing but darkness on three sides, but the wall of femurs and skulls on my left. When I press my eye to the gaps, I can see Jacob, lined with red light as his arms wrap tightly around Thomas, pinning the boy back against him.

Thomas thrashes, trying to twist free. The air around him ripples and glows red, and the whole tunnel begins to shake as the crimson light spreads over everything, splitting across the floor, the ceiling, and the walls of bone.

The poltergeist is *angry*.

I reach up, trying to haul myself out of the hole, but I can't get a grip. The sides of the hole slough away, dirt and dust and gritty stuff coming away in my hands. I can hear the sound of footsteps, the shuffle of feet, and I have the unsettling feeling that soon, we won't be alone in this section of the tunnel.

"Cass!" yelps Jacob.

"Hold on!" I call back, turning in a slow circle, trying to figure out what to do. I try to wedge my shoe in a gap, but it's no use. Up is out of the question.

The whole ground begins to shake with the force of Thomas's displeasure. Even the wall of bones to my left begins to tremble and shift.

Dad has a saying: *The only way out is through.*

I slam my shoulder into the wall, feel it shudder and slip. I hit it again, biting back a jolt of pain as the whole wall bows and leans, and finally tips and tumbles.

And falls.

The tunnel fills with the shattering sound as hundreds of dry bones crash against the dirt and stone. I spill out, coughing ash, tripping as I try to wade through the shallow tide of bones.

Jacob looks at me, eyes wide, the word unspoken but clear.

Hurry.

His hair floats in the air around him, his own eyes bright, as the boy in his arms screams and twists and fights to get free.

But Jacob doesn't let go.

I start toward them, ash dusting my skin, the mirror clenched in my hand as the walls of bone on either side sway and threaten to fall. But Thomas's eyes are still red, the photographs whipped up and torn by the whirlwind around him.

And my heart sinks, because I've tried everything, and Thomas still hasn't found his way back. Still hasn't remembered.

I don't know what to do.

But in the end, I'm not the one who does it.

Jacob's arms tighten on Thomas, and he says, *"C'est finit."*

I remember us back in the hotel room, sitting on the floor as Adele told the story of what happened to the brothers that night.

Richard called out, "Thomas, c'est finit"—"it's over"— but there was no answer, except for his own voice, echoing in the tunnels.

The red light flickers in Thomas's eyes.

The tunnel shudders, and I fight to stay on my feet. Bones crash around us, brittle as glass.

"Non," whispers Thomas, but he no longer sounds angry. Only sad, and lost.

"C'est finit, Thomas," repeats Jacob, and I swear I can see tears streaming down the dust on his face.

"C'est finit," Thomas whispers back, and the red light falters and fails.

At last, Thomas stops fighting.

The tunnel stops shaking.

The Empire of the Dead goes quiet and still.

Thomas stares up at me, his eyes wide and brown and scared as I reach him. Jacob bows his head against the boy, his eyes squeezed shut as I bring the mirror up.

"Watch and listen," I say gently.

His edges ripple in Jacob's arms.

"See and know."

He gazes into the mirror, tears staining his cheeks.

"This is what you are."

Thomas thins from flesh and blood to gossamer and smoke, and I reach into the boy's chest, fingers closing around the thread. I draw it out, the thin coil of a life that shouldn't have been so short. It comes free, dissolving in my palm, and as it disappears, so does Thomas Alain Laurent.

There, and then gone.

Poltergeist, and then ghost, and then nothing.

Jacob's arms fall to his sides, empty. He slumps back against the wall behind him, for once not even seeming to mind that it's made of skulls.

"Jacob?" I whisper, worried by his silence.

He scrubs at his eyes and swallows. Then he pulls the borrowed cap from his head and tosses it aside. "Ick," he says, peeling off the coat. "So gross."

I lean against the wall beside him, and for a long second we just sit there, amid the bones, in the dark. My head is spinning, and my throat is coated with ash, and we both know it's time to go, but something keeps us there.

"We did it," says Jacob.

"We did," I echo, leaning my head against his shoulder.

And then the Catacombs begin to whisper.

Jacob and I exchange a look.

Thomas may be gone, but this place is far from empty.

"Let's get out of here," I say, reaching for the Veil.

For an instant, it resists, but then Jacob's hand joins mine, and together we pass through. A surge of cold hits my lungs, and the world is back, and suddenly bright. A second later, Jacob appears beside me, his usual see-through self, and I look around, worried we've wandered too far. But then I hear my parents' voices, loud and blessedly close, and I round the corner the instant before they turn back and look.

"There you are," calls Dad. "I thought we warned you not to wander."

"Sorry," I say, jogging to catch up. "I was trying to stay out of the shots."

Mom slings an arm around my shoulder.

She looks back into the Catacombs.

"Here's hoping that's the end of that," she says.

And I couldn't agree more.

We climb in silence, and it's only when we reach the street that Mom notices my clothes.

"Cassidy Blake," she scolds. "How on earth did you get so dirty?"

CHAPTER TWENTY-SEVEN

Back at the Hotel Valeur, I take a really, *really* hot shower, trying to rinse the Catacombs from my skin. I towel off and slide on a pair of red-and-yellow pajamas, feeling like I've earned my Gryffindor colors tonight.

Mom and Dad are on the sofa, sharing a bottle of red wine as they watch the new footage. Annette gave them a copy of the digital file only, and said it would be best if she and Anton looked after the rest.

On the screen, my parents stand before a wall of bones, the lights casting long shadows across each of the patterned skulls.

"Looks good," I say, padding past them.

"Well," says Dad, "it wasn't how we planned on spending our last night—"

"But the upside is," adds Mom, "this take turned out even better."

"I'm glad it all worked out," I say, genuinely relieved.

"Want to watch?" asks Mom, patting the sofa beside her, where Grim twitches an ear.

I shake my head. "No thanks," I say.

I've officially had enough of the Empire of the Dead.

In my room, I find Jacob sitting on the sill of the open window.

He glances over his shoulder.

"I wish *I* could take a shower," he says, rubbing at a smudge of dirt on his arm. "I smell like grave dirt and old bones."

I cross to the window beside him and sniff the air. "You don't smell like anything to me."

"Well, clearly *my* spectral senses are sharper than yours." He runs a hand through his hair. "Speaking of smells, now that Thomas is gone, can we please get rid of all the sage and salt? It's giving me a wicked headache."

"Sure thing." I search the hotel room and find the pouches I've hidden in Mom and Dad's bags, on their windowsills, under the sofa, and in the planter by the door.

"What are you doing, Cass?" asks Mom as I put the box of protective charms out in the hall.

"Just packing," I say, returning to my room.

"Better?" I ask.

Jacob sighs in relief. "Much," he says, but he doesn't climb down from the open window. Something's clearly still bothering him, and I want to ask, but I don't. I have to trust him, to believe that if he's ready to tell me what he's thinking, he will.

So instead I slump back on the bed, wincing as something digs into my side.

My cell phone.

I forgot to turn it back on, and when I do, my screen fills with messages, every one of them from Lara Chowdhury.

Lara:
How did it go?

Lara:
Cassidy?

Lara:
If you die, I will hunt down your ghost.

Lara:
Hello?

Lara:
You'd better be okay.

I text her back, promising that I'm all right, that Thomas

Laurent has officially been sent on (making a point that I couldn't have done it without Jacob's help), and that I'll explain everything tomorrow. Tonight I just want to sleep.

I sag back against the pillows and close my eyes, already sinking down into the dark.

I wake up once in the middle of the night.

No nightmare this time, just the feeling that I'm not alone. I roll over in bed and see Jacob still sitting there, in the open window, his head tipped back. He's got that faraway look, like he's staring past the city buildings to somewhere I can't see. Maybe I'm still asleep, maybe *this* is the dream, because he doesn't seem to hear me when I think his name. I close my eyes, and the next thing I know, it's morning.

Sunlight streams through the windows as we pack up our things. We drop off the luggage and Grim's cat carrier at the front desk, much to the clerk's displeasure.

It's our last morning, and there's still one thing I have to do.

"Couldn't you just call her?" asks Dad when I tell him my plan.

I shake my head. "I still have her photos," I say. "Besides, I want to say goodbye."

Mom rests a hand on my shoulder. "It's all right," she says. "We have time."

Outside, it's a gorgeous day, and the whole city shines with light, from the pale stone buildings to the metal rooftops rising against the bright blue sky. And Paris seems to be returning to normal. The Metro is running, the streetlights have stopped shorting out, and there are no emergency vehicles whistling past.

It's like Thomas never happened.

But of course, he did.

And even if this city is already moving on, I'm not likely to forget anytime soon.

When we get to the Laurents' building, I ask Mom and Dad to wait outside, and take the stairs two at a time up to apartment 3A. Madame Laurent answers, and at the sight of me standing on her front mat, her eyes narrow, instantly suspicious.

"You again?" she asks, her hand tightening on the open door, but Adele appears at her side.

"*Maman!* She's a friend."

They exchange a few words of rapid French. Then Sylvaine sighs and retreats, leaving Adele and me (and Jacob) alone in the doorway. Adele is dressed in the same gold sneakers and jeans, along with a red-and-yellow sweatshirt, the house emblem over her heart.

Of course. She's a Gryffindor.

"Come," she says brightly, "let's go to my room."

Adele leads me down the hall and into a bright little bedroom.

"Did it work?" she asks as soon as the door is closed. "What was it like?"

I glance at Jacob, but for once, he looks away.

"It was intense," I say. "But in the end, we got through to him. Thomas remembered who he was, and I was able to send him on."

Adele nods thoughtfully. "Where do you think he went?"

"That's a really big question," I say. "And to be honest, I don't know. Somewhere we can't follow. But the important thing is, he's not trapped anymore. And he's not lost. He's free."

Adele smiles. "Good," she says. "Thank you, Cassidy."

"I couldn't have done it without your help," I say. I look to Jacob. *And yours.*

Jacob manages a sad smile but says nothing—he's still acting strange.

Adele plucks a lollipop from a jar by the chest of drawers and offers me one. I take it, unwrapping a bright yellow candy. Lemon.

"I never liked lemon," says Jacob, even though I know he's just sulking because he can't eat sugar.

"More for me," I say absently.

Adele's eyes widen. "Were you talking to Jacob?" She looks around. "Is he here with us?"

And Jacob, in response, reaches out and raps his knuckles on the windowpane. It gives a tiny shudder, like a pebble hitting glass.

Adele whips around, and I watch, half-amused, half-concerned, as Jacob fogs the window and draws his finger through the mist. A smiley face.

Adele beams. "So cool."

"Anyway," I say, pulling the photos from my camera bag. "I wanted to bring these back. I'm sorry they got a little dirty."

That's an understatement.

One has a dusty shoe print. Another is torn almost in two.

Adele takes the photos, pressing them to her chest.

"Thank you," she says, before digging the pouch of sage and salt from her pocket. "I should give this back," she says, holding it out.

"Keep it," I say.

"Yeah," adds Jacob, sniffling.

Adele smiles and puts the pouch away.

"I guess this is goodbye," I say.

"No," says Adele. *"À bientôt."*

"What does that mean?"

"See you soon."

She smiles, and I have the strange feeling she's right.

I find Mom and Dad across the street, sitting at an outdoor café, drinking coffee and eating croissants. Jacob trails a step behind me. He's been quiet all morning.

Though the truth is, he's been quiet since the Catacombs last night. Since even before that. I know he can hear me wondering, worrying about his silence, but he doesn't offer an answer, and I force myself not to ask. He'll talk about it when he's ready. I hope.

I sink into the chair across from Mom and Dad, and reach for the last bite of croissant on Mom's plate. She snatches it before I can get there and pops the bite into her mouth with a wicked smile. Then she hands me a paper bag with an entire pain au chocolat inside.

I grin. *"Merci,"* I say around a mouthful of pastry.

Dad checks the time on his phone. "We have one more place to go."

I'm confused. "But the film crew is gone. I thought we were done."

"This isn't for the show," says Mom. "No Inspecters today. We can just be a normal family."

At that, Jacob's mouth finally crooks into a faint smile as he whispers:

*"Para*normal."

CHAPTER TWENTY-EIGHT

Y ou can't go to Paris without seeing the Louvre,"
says Mom as we cross the palace courtyard. "It's
simply not allowed."

That's where we're going: the Louvre, that big museum
marked by the glass pyramid at the end of the Tuileries.

This place is *massive*. There are whole wings dedicated
to different countries, different periods of time. There are
statues and paintings, tapestries and tiles, sculptures and
antiques. Fragments of the past. It would take weeks, maybe
even years to see everything, but we only have a couple of
hours, so we jump from one exhibit to the next with all
the other tourists. In one room, a large crowd gathers
around a tiny painting, and when we get close enough, I
see that it's the *Mona Lisa*. I always thought it would be
bigger.

Jacob walks next to me, not really looking at the art

but past it, through it, somewhere else. For the hundredth time, I wish I could read his mind the way he reads mine.

As we head downstairs, I can feel the *tap-tap-tap* of ghosts. The Veil ripples around me, but it's not until we reach the Egypt wing that I learn why.

"Do you see those marks?" asks Mom, gesturing to the inside of a sarcophagus. "Those are from a person's nails." She waggles her fingers. "It means they were entombed *before* they were dead."

"Nope," says Jacob, and I have to agree with him, grateful when we move on to a hall of marble statues.

"It's important to take care of the past," muses Dad as we walk between exhibits. "To revisit it, to study and learn. Understanding the past helps us move through the present and discover the future."

And remembering the past helps us move on, I think. *Helps us let go.*

Jacob begins to fall behind, first one step, then two. Until I look over my shoulder and see that he's not there. My parents, arm in arm, stop to examine a statue, and I drift away from them, promising I'll be right back. For once, they let me go.

I find Jacob, sitting on a bench on the other side of the

room. He's staring at piece of stone inside a case, the carvings on its face worn away to almost nothing.

"Hey," I say, coming to stand beside him.

"Hey," he echoes, keeping his gaze ahead.

He's quiet for a long moment, and then he lets out a shuddering breath.

"Cass," he says slowly. "I'm ready to tell you."

"Tell me what?"

"What happened to me."

I stiffen. I've always *wanted* to know, but I also accepted the fact that Jacob didn't want to share. I couldn't blame him for that, not really—who wants to think about the way they died, what they lost?

"Are you sure?"

His voice, when he answers, is so low I barely hear. "Yeah."

He looks down at his hands on his knees, and we both see it—the way his fingers rest on his jeans. He's not as transparent as he used to be.

"Jacob," I say. "If you're not ready, you don't have to—"

But he cuts me off. "I still remember. But I also know the only difference between me and Thomas is the fact I haven't forgotten yet."

"But that's *not* the only difference," I remind him. "*You* also have *me*."

"Exactly," says Jacob. "That's why I'm telling you. So that if I ever start to forget, you can help me remember."

I exhale shakily. "Okay," I say. "I'm listening."

He runs both hands through his hair, links them behind his head. It's a pose I've seen him strike a hundred times, but his face has never looked like this. Serious and sad.

I can't help but think of the boy I saw in the shards of mirror, the other version of Jacob, lost and gray and floating. But this Jacob is different. He's right here beside me, his eyes closed, his brow creased, his whole body tensed against the truth, even as he says it.

"Ellis Hale."

"Who's that?" I ask.

"Me." His eyes drift open. "I mean, that's my name, the rest of it. Jacob Ellis Hale."

Jacob Ellis Hale.

It's so weird, but those two extra names, they make him seem . . . real. Which is insane, because Jacob's always seemed real to me. But I've also only ever known him as he is now, with his messy blond hair and his superhero shirt and his jeans, constant, unchanging—

"Dead," he finishes for me.

It's the first time I've ever heard him use that word, and he scrunches his face up a little as he says it, as if it tastes bad.

"I was born in Strathclyde—that's in upstate New York—but we moved to Landing when I was eight."

Landing—that's the town right next to mine, the one on the other side of the river.

"Eight hundred and fifty-seven days. That's how long ago it happened, if you keep track. Which I do."

I don't have to tell him that I keep track, too, that I count every day from the one I (almost) drowned. For me, that number is 392. I'm not even sure I try to keep track; I just wake up every day knowing.

As for Jacob, I do the math in my head, or at least I try—I've never been all that good at math—and I'm still trying to carry the one when he says, "Two and a half years."

Two and a half years.

That means, if he were still alive, he'd be almost fifteen.

I knew he was older than me—he had to be. After all, we're the same age, but he died before I drowned.

"For what it's worth," he says, "I don't *feel* any older. Maybe it's the whole ghost thing."

"Maybe boys just mature slower," I tease.

He smiles weakly.

"Sorry," I say. "Go on."

He takes a slow, steadying breath. "Anyway, me and my brothers—"

Brothers. Family. My mind goes to Thomas and Richard, to the strange weight that's been hanging in the air around Jacob ever since we learned the truth of Thomas's story.

"You have brothers?"

"Yeah." A new light comes into his eyes then. His smile is sad and sweet at the same time. "Two of them. Matthew, he was sixteen, though I guess he's older now. Probably off in college. And Kit, well, Kit drove me crazy. He was only seven when . . ."

Jacob lets out a low breath, then inhales deeply, as if he's about to dive into deep water.

"Kit had this action figure he loved, Skull from *Skull and Bones*. I gave it to him for his seventh birthday, and he took it everywhere. To school. To bed. Even in the shower." He laughs softly. "So we were at the river, and of course Kit had the action figure there, too. I told him not to take it into the water. I told him he'd lose it. But little brothers . . ." He shakes his head. "They don't always listen. All it took was one good wave, and Kit lost that stupid toy.

"I was swimming when it happened. I came up for air and saw him sitting on the bank, sobbing. I got out, thought he must be hurt or something. He was so upset. Threw a wicked tantrum. So I did what I had to do. I dove back in."

I close my eyes as he talks, and it's weird, but I swear I can see it—the river, quick-flowing in summer. Jacob's little brother, his knees drawn up on the bank. I don't know if it's just my imagination, or because we're connected, but if it's the second, this is the first time our mental link has gone both ways.

The first time I've seen into Jacob's head.

The first time he's let me.

"The action figure was heavy," he explains. "It had these weights in it, so you could make it walk along the bottom of a bathtub, that kind of thing. So I knew it was probably somewhere on the bottom of the river. It took three or four dives before I saw it, but when I dove down to get it, it was wedged under a stick or something. Took me a few seconds to get it free, and I almost had it when . . ." He clears his throat. "I don't know, Cass. To this day, I really don't. The current must have picked up. It did that sometimes. Churned up rocks and logs, sent them sailing low along the river floor. All I know is something hit me, something hard, and the world just . . . stopped."

Jacob swallows hard. "And that was that."

Four small words.

The difference between life and death. My head spins, reeling. I don't know what to say, but I have to say something, and I know better than to say something like *sorry*.

I've only ever known Jacob the Ghost. What that really means is that I've only known Jacob from the point when he entered *my* story. I didn't think so much about the fact that he had a story of his own. A whole life, short as it was, before we got tangled up, before he became my best friend.

Now it's like he's filling out in front of me, becoming solid. Alive.

"Did you ever try to go back to them?" I whisper.

"You're asking me if I haunted my family?" Jacob grits his teeth. "No. I . . . couldn't. Not at first. I couldn't leave the river."

Of course. It was his Veil.

"And then, after I met you, and I *could* leave . . . I was— I guess I was afraid of seeing them without me. Afraid it would hurt too much. Afraid I would get stuck there. Like the Mirror of Erisorn."

I stifle a laugh. "Erised." That's the mirror in Harry Potter that shows someone what they want most, but Dumbledore warned Harry that people could waste away in front of it.

Jacob manages a small smile. "Yeah. Like that." He looks down. "I really should read those books."

"You really should."

We both go quiet after that.

Jacob is done talking, and I don't know what to say. I'm sad I didn't know before. I'm glad that I do now. That he's trusted me with this, his past, his truth, the pieces that add up to Jacob. And no matter what happens, I won't let him forget who he was, who he is. What he means to me.

I lean against him, just until the air blurs between our shoulders, and this time, when I feel the slight resistance of his body against mine, it doesn't scare me.

Your name is Jacob Ellis Hale, I think. *You were born in Strathclyde, New York. Two and half years ago you dove into the river, and last year, you pulled me out.*

You are my best friend.

In life. In death.

And everything in between.

CHAPTER TWENTY-NINE

Pauline is waiting for us back at the hotel, sitting on a plush seat beside our luggage and Grim's carrier.

She stands when she sees us, elegant as ever in a white outfit and dark heels. She hands me a small parcel. My photos, developed by her father.

"Monsieur Deschamp sends his regards," she says. "He says you have a special eye, and that you must have used some clever techniques to get the effects you did."

I press the envelope to my chest. The truth is, I have no idea if my camera still works, if the magic lay in a specific part, like the original lens I lost. Or if it's special because it's mine.

Only one way to find out.

I turn through the photos as Mom and Dad check out of the hotel.

Among the "normal" photos is a shot of Mom and Dad in the Tuileries our first night, the carnival rising in the background, the light blurring faintly so it looks like fire. Then a picture of the two of them standing on a narrow street, admiring a window full of macarons. The crew setting up among the crypts in Père Lachaise, and Mom on a bench, hands spread as she speaks in the Jardin du Luxembourg. The opera, with its gleaming chandelier before it fell. A photo of Adele, beaming around the white stick of a lollipop on our way to Notre-Dame. And of course, our first trip to the Catacombs, the empty gallery leading to the tombs, and then the tunnels and tunnels of bones.

I'm proud of these pictures. They're exactly what Mom and Dad asked for, a look behind the scenes at the making of their show.

But the paranormal shots, the ones I took *beyond* the Veil, are something else. Something more. I was afraid that the new lens wouldn't work, but the magic of my camera clearly doesn't belong to any one piece.

If anything, the images are getting clearer.

The Tuileries, the Catacombs, the cemetery at Père Lachaise—they show up in ghostly shades of gray, the images faint, underexposed but visible. The palace, traced with white from the searing heat of the fire. The tunnels, dark save for the faint glow of a lantern, the empty gaze of a skull.

There's also the series of shots I took from the bedroom window of my hotel room when Thomas appeared on the street below. I remember him vividly, standing there, his red eyes tipped up. In the photo, though, the street looks empty, the sidewalk marked only by the ghost of a ghost of a ghost, a shadow against shadows, so faint no one else would know.

And then there's the photo I took of Jacob, sitting atop the broken angel in Père Lachaise. The statue is striking in black and white, but the air over its shoulder is hardly empty. Instead, it bends like candle smoke, like the after-image of a flash when you blink, ghosted onto the mottled branches between the tombstone and the sky.

It forms the shape of a boy, one knee drawn up, his face caught in the motion of turning away.

There's no question, Jacob is getting clearer, too.

He moves toward me, and I tuck the photographs back in the folder before he reaches me. Pauline is coming, too. She kisses me twice, once on each cheek.

"It was nice to meet you, Cassidy."

"Well, Pauline," asks Dad, "did we make a believer out of you?"

She glances at me, her mouth drawing into a small smile. "Perhaps," she says. "I will admit, there's more to this world than meets the eye."

We gather up our things, say goodbye to the Hotel Valeur (and the desk clerk, who seems particularly glad to see us go), and step out into the Paris sun.

As we make our way to the Metro, I can't help but look down at the sidewalk and remember how much history, how many secrets, is buried beneath our feet.

"If you had to sum up Paris in one word," says Mom, "what would it be?"

Dad considers, then says, "Overwhelming."

"Enchanted," counters Mom.

"Haunted," offers Jacob dryly.

I think for a moment, but in the end, I find the perfect word.

"Unforgettable."

As we wait for the train to the airport, Jacob wanders up and down the platform. I watch as he amuses himself by bobbing a child's balloon, putting his hand through a musician's amp as they lean against a pillar, playing guitar. He seems happier, lighter, after sharing his story. I feel a little heavier after hearing it, but that's okay. That's how friendship works. You learn to share the weight.

I stick my hands in the pockets of my jeans and feel the edge of something solid and square. I draw it out and freeze. It's the data card I stole from the footage case, the one marked CAT for Catacombs. My heart thuds as I look over at Mom and Dad, who are standing together and talking a few feet away. I walk over to the nearest trash can, dropping the card inside.

That's when I notice the man.

He's standing on the opposite platform, the gulf of the tracks between us, and the first thing I notice is how still he is amid the sea of people.

He looks like a thin shadow in a black suit. He wears white gloves and a black hat with a brim that covers his face.

Until he raises his head, and then I see it isn't a face at all but a mask. Smooth and white as bone. And a shiver runs through me, because the contours and angles are the same I saw a thousand times down in the Catacombs.

The mask is a skull.

Somewhere behind the open sockets there must be eyes, but I can't see them. It's as if he's wearing a second mask under the first, one that's solid black, erasing all his features.

My fingers go to the camera around my neck. I can't take my eyes off him.

He's so out of place amid the tourists with their suitcases and summer clothes that at first I think the man must be a street performer, one of those who stand perfectly still until you drop a coin into their bowl. But if he's performing, nobody seems to notice. In fact, the people on the platform move around the man like water around a rock. As if they don't even *see* him.

But I do.

"Jacob," I whisper, but he's too far away.

I raise the camera to snap a shot, but as I do, the man looks at me. He lifts a gloved hand to his mask, and suddenly I can't move. My limbs are frozen, my legs dead weight, and as he pulls the mask from his face, all I see is darkness.

My vision flickers, and my lungs flood with cold water.

The Metro disappears and the platform falls away beneath my feet and I fall, plunging down, down into the icy dark.

Everything is gone.

And then it's back. The world fills with sound, worried voices, fluorescent light. I'm on the ground, gasping, and I feel like I'm about to spit up river water. But there's only air, and the cold hard surface of the platform beneath me.

Jacob is kneeling on one side of me, and Dad is on the other, helping me sit up. Mom is punching a number into her phone, her face awash in fear. I've never seen her afraid. Not seriously. Other people are gathering, murmuring to themselves in quiet French, and I blush, suddenly self-conscious.

"What happened?" I ask.

"You fainted," says Dad.

"Dropped like a stone," adds Jacob.

Like the ground was gone.

Like I was falling.

"There's no signal," mutters Mom, her eyes glassy with tears.

"I think she's okay," says Dad, putting his hand on her arm before turning back to me. "Hey, kiddo. You all right?"

I get to my feet, and Mom wraps her arms around me. I spend the next couple of minutes assuring my parents (and Jacob) that I'm okay, that I just got light-headed, that I'm more embarrassed than hurt. And that last part, at least, is true. There's a dull ache where my knee hit the ground, and a bad feeling in my chest.

Then I remember. I stiffen, my eyes going instantly back to the place where the shadow stood on the opposite platform. But the man in the black suit with the wide brim hat and the skull mask is gone.

I swallow, the taste of the river still in my throat. Jacob follows my gaze across the platform, reading my thoughts, my questions.

Did you see him? I ask.

Jacob shakes his head. "Who was he?"

I'm . . . not sure.

But whoever the guy was, he's gone, and so is the faint, dizzy feeling. And yeah, that was weird. But it's not the weirdest thing to happen to me this year . . . or this month . . . or this week.

Mom and Dad are still studying me, shooting me nervous looks, ready to catch me if I fall. But I feel fine now. Really, I do. I make a note to tell Lara about it later.

By the time the train pulls into the station, the whole thing feels like a dream, far away, just as silly and just as strange. I put it away, in the back of my mind, as the train doors open and we climb aboard. The Blake family: two parents, a ghost-seeing girl, her dead best friend, and a rather unhappy cat.

Jacob perches on a piece of luggage, I lean against Mom, and Dad rests a hand on my head as the train doors slide shut on the platform, and on Paris.

The train pulls out of the station into the dark tunnel, and I adjust the camera on my shoulder, excited to see what happens next.

ABOUT THE AUTHOR

Victoria (V. E.) Schwab is the #1 *New York Times* bestselling author of more than a dozen novels for young adults and adults, including *City of Ghosts*, the Shades of Magic series, *Vicious*, *Vengeful*, *This Savage Song*, and *Our Dark Duet*. Victoria can often be found haunting Paris streets and trudging up Scottish hillsides. Usually, she's tucked in the corner of a coffee shop, dreaming up stories. Visit her online at veschwab.com.

READ HOW CASS AND JACOB'S ADVENTURES ALL BEGAN!

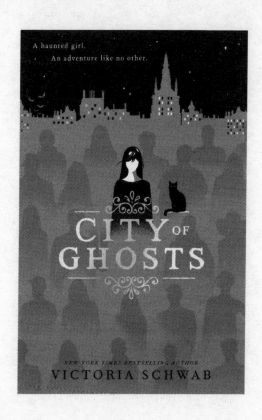